I0542413

Pride Publishing books by Carol Lynne:

Campus Cravings Volume One: On the Field
Coach
Side-Lined
Sacking the Quarterback

Campus Cravings Volume Two: Off the Field
Off Season
Forbidden Freshman

Campus Cravings Volume Three: Back on Campus
Broken Pottery
In Bear's Bed

Campus Cravings Volume Four: Dorm Life
Office Advances
A Biker's Vow

Campus Cravings Volume Five: BK House
Hershie's Kiss
Theron's Return

Campus Cravings Volume Six
Incoming Freshman
A Lesson Learned

Campus Cravings
Live for Today

Campus Cravings Volume Seven
Locky in Love
The Injustice of Being

Campus Cravings Volume Eight
Watch Me
Coming Clean

Campus Cravings Volume Nine
Professor Sandwich
Big Man on Campus

Good-Time Boys
Sonny's Salvation
Garron's Gift
Rawley's Redemption
Twin Temptations
It's a Good Life

Cattle Valley Volume One
All Play & No Work
Cattle Valley Mistletoe

Cattle Valley Volume Two
Sweet Topping
Rough Ride

Cattle Valley Volume Three
Physical Therapy
Out of the Shadow

Cattle Valley Volume Four
Bad Boy Cowboy
The Sound of White

Cattle Valley Volume Five
Gone Surfin'
The Last Bouquet

Cattle Valley Volume Six
Eye of the Beholder
Cattle Valley Days

Cattle Valley Volume Seven
Bent— Not Broken
Arm Candy

Cattle Valley Volume Eight
Recipe for Love
Firehouse Heat

Men in Love
Reunion

Bodyguards in Love Volume One
Brier's Bargain
Seb's Surrender

Bodyguards in Love Volume Two
I Love Rock N Roll
Taming Black Dog Four

Bodyguards in Love Volume Three
Seducing the Sheik
To Bed a King

Seasons of Love Volume One
Spring

Seasons of Love Volume Two
Summer
Fall

Seasons of Love Volume Three
Winter

Brookside Athletic Club Volume One
I'll Stand By You
Soul Restoration

Neo's Realm Volume One
Liquid Crimson
Blood Trinity

Neo's Realm Volume Two
Crimson Moon
Royal Blood

C-7 Shifters
Alrik
Seger

CAMPUS CRAVINGS
Volume Nine

Professor Sandwich

Big Man on Campus

CAROL LYNNE

Campus Cravings Volume Nine
ISBN # 978-1-78430-716-5
©Copyright Carol Lynne 2015
Cover Art by Posh Gosh ©Copyright August 2015
Interior text design by Claire Siemaszkiewicz
Pride Publishing

Published in 2015 by Pride Publishing, Newland House, The Point, Weaver Road, Lincoln, LN6 3QN, United Kingdom.

Pride Publishing is a subsidiary of Totally Entwined Group Limited.

PROFESSOR SANDWICH

Dedication

Thanks to my fellow GRL Retreat organizers, Ethan Day, Teresa Emil and Reese Dante, I was able to hand off a few of my organizing duties in order to get this story completed. I know it's a give and take in the world of unpaid event organizing, and I want to thank the three of you for giving me the gift of time.

Prologue

Even though he'd only had one glass of wine, Rusty Bonham was proud of himself for staying at Clean Slate as long as he had. He'd never liked crowds and he'd quickly discovered they were even worse in a gay bar full of horny men. His ass still hurt from all the anonymous hands that had groped and pinched him as he'd tried to work his way through the throng of people to get to his roommate's table.

Chase's new boyfriend, Mac, was hot, so Rusty understood Chase's desire to go to the bar, but once Chase and Mac had started making out right in front of him, Rusty had known he needed to be somewhere else. He'd excused himself to go to the restroom and that was when he'd seen them. Professors Adam Ryan and Manuel Corto Delgado were seated at a small table near the restrooms. Rusty's heart had lurched at the sight of them, smiling and talking only to each other. Watching them together had taken him back to the night his parents had been killed in an automobile accident. It'd been Professor Ryan who'd rushed to BK House, the dorm Rusty lived in. The professor had held Rusty for hours until Rusty had finally fallen asleep.

Restroom forgotten, he went back to his table to grab his coat. He let Chase know he was leaving, giving him a lame excuse about homework he needed to finish. In actuality, he couldn't handle the sight of the professors and their blissful happiness.

After braving the pinching crowd, Rusty finally stepped out of the club and into the parking lot. He reached into his coat pocket for his keys and wondered how he could've been stupid enough to think Professor Ryan had really liked him. Not like a teacher likes a student but like a man likes another man. *Yep, stupid.* There had been rumors floating around about a sexual relationship between Professors Ryan and Corto Delgado, but Rusty hadn't wanted to believe them. Unfortunately, seeing the way Professor Ryan stared into the visiting Spanish professor's eyes had left no doubt in Rusty's mind the two men were sleeping together.

"That's him!" a loud voice yelled.

Rusty wheeled toward the noise and was immediately blindsided by a fist. His head jerked back on impact, glasses falling from his face. Before he could right himself, another punch caught him in the jaw, knocking him to the ground. He blinked and stared up at the man, but his face was weird, as if he was wearing a mask.

"Hey!" someone screamed. "Get away from him!"

"Let's go," his attacker snarled. He and another faceless man who'd been standing nearby took off toward a dark car. Before disappearing, the man in the black ski mask turned back to Rusty. "We'll be back."

Dazed, Rusty frantically searched the ground for his glasses as a small crowd of people began to surround him. "Stay back," he begged, holding his hands up to ward off another blow.

"It's cool, man. A guy already called the cops," a man responded. He pressed something cold into Rusty's hand. "They're broken."

Rusty curled his hand around the glasses as he continued to crab-walk backward toward his car. He felt wetness on his cheek, but he didn't dare take his eyes off the people staring down at him until his spine hit the cold metal of his car.

"Rusty," Professor Ryan soothed in a deep voice as he knelt beside Rusty. He tilted Rusty's head to the side. "Fuck." He glanced up. "He needs a doctor."

Professor Corto Delgado moved to kneel on the opposite side of Rusty. He pulled a white handkerchief from his back pocket and dabbed at the cut on Rusty's cheek. "What happened?" he asked in a heavy Spanish accent.

Rusty stared down at his broken glasses, unable to speak. How was he going to study if he couldn't see his textbooks? He leaned back against his car and closed his eyes. It wasn't the first time his glasses had been broken by a bully. Hell, it wasn't even the second or third time, so he had no idea why he was surprised by the attack.

Chase cleared his throat and Professor Corto Delgado stood and took a step back. Chase lowered himself beside Rusty. "Hey."

Rusty glanced up from his glasses to regard Chase. "I don't have a spare pair," he mumbled.

"There's one of those glasses in an hour places at the mall. I can take you in the morning," Chase said.

"But I need to study tonight," Rusty countered, returning his gaze to the broken frames. He couldn't remember a time when he hadn't worn glasses. From what he'd been told, his parents had known soon after he was born that his eyesight wasn't right.

Chase reached out and tilted Rusty's chin up. "Do you need to go to the hospital?"

Rusty's eyes filled with tears. "It's been a long time since I've been beaten up. I forgot how much it hurts."

"Yeah, it does," Chase agreed.

Rusty felt bad for saying it, knowing his roommate was remembering the times when his father had beat him and his mother as a child.

"We should get him to the emergency room," Professor Corto Delgado said.

"What about the police?" Chase asked.

"They're taking their sweet time," Professor Ryan ground out between clenched teeth. "As far as I'm concerned, they can talk to Rusty either tomorrow or at the hospital."

Chase gently took the glasses from Rusty. "Why don't you let the professors take you to get checked out? At the least, I think you might need a stitch or two to close the cut on your cheek. I'll be there as soon as I can."

Rusty stared at Chase. "I'll have a scar like yours."

Chase absently brushed the crescent-shaped scar on his cheekbone. "You're right, you will."

Rusty closed his eyes. When he was a child, his mom had cleaned his wounds while whispering words of love and support. God, he missed her every day. Despite the fact that he hadn't lived with his family for years, he missed the feeling they were only a phone call away. "I wish I could talk to my mom."

Chase pulled the scarf from around his neck and used it to dab at the blood dripping down Rusty's face. "You can talk to me."

Rusty glanced up at Professor Ryan, wishing he had a right to cling to the professor again. Unfortunately, that honor belonged to Manuel. He returned his gaze to Chase. "Maybe."

Chase glanced from Rusty to Professor Ryan. "Go ahead and take him to the hospital." He held up Rusty's glasses. "I'll keep these for now."

Professor Corto Delgado scooped Rusty off the pavement and into his muscular arms. Knowing it was wrong, Rusty couldn't help but melt against the safety and warmth of the professor's chest. Before they could get far, the police arrived. Manuel growled low in his throat. Still carrying Rusty, the professor walked over to one of the cops. "I'm taking him to the hospital. If you want to talk to him, meet us there."

The police officer started to argue but was soon distracted by another call coming in on his radio.

"Let's go," Professor Ryan said.

Manuel rested his cheek against Rusty's hair as he carried him across the parking lot. He stopped in front of a sleek black sedan and surprised Rusty with a soft kiss on his forehead. "Can you reach the keys in my pocket?"

"Which one?" Rusty asked as his heart pounded. The thought of being so close to the sexy man's cock made him nervous.

The professor grinned at Rusty. "Left coat." He winked.

Rusty reached inside the coat and withdrew the keys. He held them up.

"You drive," Manuel told Professor Ryan.

"I'll hold him. You can drive," Professor Ryan argued.

"I've already got him." Manuel leaned over and brushed his lips across Professor Ryan's mouth. "Let me."

Rusty's heart squeezed at the soft expression on Professor Corto Delgado's face. It was obvious the two men loved each other, so why were they being so nice to him? The last thing he wanted was to cause problems. "I can sit in the back by myself," he volunteered.

Professor Ryan took the keys from Rusty's hand. "That's not necessary." He smoothed the back of his finger over Rusty's cheek just below the cut. He shook his head and took a deep breath before unlocking the car.

Professor Corto Delgado opened the back driver's side door and climbed in with Rusty still in his arms.

Rusty eyed the interior of the car. *Damn.* He had no idea what kind of car it was, but it had luxury written all over it. "Professor, I'm fine to sit in the other seat."

Professor Corto Delgado held him tighter. "You're fine where you are." He kissed the top of Rusty's head again. "And call me Manuel or Manny, whichever you're more comfortable with."

Rusty tilted his chin up and studied the handsome Spaniard. Despite everything appearing fuzzy without his glasses, he could still make out the professor's face. With short, midnight black hair and the darkest brown eyes Rusty had ever seen, the man was movie-star gorgeous. He liked the thought of calling the professor Manny, but it sounded too familiar. "Manuel."

"And call me Adam," Professor Ryan said from behind the wheel. He eased the sedan out of the parking lot and passed the gathered group of people who were still milling around. "I was shocked to see you at the bar," he said.

Rusty cringed. He knew he looked like he was a kid, but he wasn't. "I'm twenty-two."

Adam chuckled. "No, I just meant I've never seen you out before."

"That was my first and last time." Rusty leaned his head against Manuel. "Of all the people there, why'd they choose me?"

"I think you were at the wrong place at the wrong time, *bebé*." Manuel dabbed at the cut on Rusty's cheek with the handkerchief he'd used earlier.

"No." Rusty shook his head. "I heard one of them say *that's him*. It was like they were waiting for me."

"Did you recognize the voices? Maybe you know them?" Manuel asked.

"I don't know who they were, but they didn't sound like anyone my age," Rusty replied.

Adam took a left into the hospital's drive and stopped outside the emergency room. "Take him in, and I'll park the car." He turned in his seat and touched Rusty's leg. "Don't worry. We'll take care of you."

Manuel opened the door and easily got out of the car with Rusty still in his arms. Rusty rested his head against Manuel's muscled chest and began to worry for a different reason.

* * * *

A noise startled Rusty from an uneasy sleep. He gasped and jackknifed into a sitting position. Breathing still erratic, he looked around at the unfamiliar surroundings. It took him a frantic moment to remember he was safely ensconced in Manuel's guestroom.

He flopped back down to his pillow before wiping the light sheen of sweat from his forehead. Lights from the city outside the floor to ceiling window danced across the room, creating interesting shadows as he dissected his dream. Unlike the bullies who'd attacked him regularly in the past, the man who'd jumped him in the parking lot of Clean Slate hadn't verbally abused him. There had been no taunting names like fag, Icky or ass-licker, God, he'd hated that last one. He knew the cops, the people at the bar and even the professors believed it was a hate crime against gays, but something in his gut told him it had nothing to do with his sexual orientation.

A loud thump shook Rusty from his thoughts. He sat up again, prepared to run if the man in the mask had returned for him. The guest bedroom he'd used since the professors had literally carried him home with them the previous night was closest to the front door. Jesus, Mary and Joseph, what was he supposed to do, hide?

Rusty glanced around the large guestroom. Like most of the luxury apartment, the room was modern and incredibly minimalist in furnishings. The platform bed made it impossible to hide under and he'd seen enough horror movies to know the closet was always the worst place to go. *Shoot.*

He eyed the open door. The master bedroom was down the hall in the opposite direction of the front door. *Safety in numbers.* Dressed in only a pair of boxers, he slid along the wall toward the hallway.

The thump sounded again, prompting him to move faster. Heart in his throat, he darted out of the bedroom and down the hall toward the safety of the professors. Manuel's door was open a crack, and Rusty lifted his hand to push it open when that darn noise came again. He stilled when he realized the noise was coming from inside the room.

"*Joder, mi cielo. Te sientes tan bien,*" Manuel's deep voice growled.

Fuck, my heaven. You feel so good. Rusty closed his eyes, grateful he'd become fluent in Spanish.

Another thump and Rusty couldn't stop himself from pushing the door open enough to see what the heck was making the noise. His hand flew to cover his mouth as he spotted the professors.

With his legs wrapped around Manuel's waist, Adam was pressed against the wall of glass as Manuel fucked him hard. A litany of Spanish phrases slipped from Manuel's lips as he continued to pound into Adam, and it took all of Rusty's skill to translate them in his head as his hand wandered down to his tented boxers.

"*Tu eres muy sexy.*" *You are very sexy.* "*Bésame.*" *Kiss me.* "*Tu me vuelves loco!*" *You drive me crazy.*

Rusty leaned against the doorframe as he watched the sweat-slicked bodies writhe against each other with the glow of the city lights as their backdrop. It was the most erotic thing he'd ever witnessed. He wrapped his hand around his cock and squeezed. Although he'd known he preferred males from a very early age, he still had never so much as kissed another man.

"Yes! Harder," Adam moaned.

Manuel pulled out before slamming back inside. The resulting thump as Adam's spine connected with the window gave Rusty his answer. Rusty worked his hand up and down his erection as he continued to peer into the private lives of the two men. He couldn't stop the groan of pleasure that escaped him. *Darn it!*

He held his breath as he took a step back, and prayed he hadn't been heard.

"You can come in," Adam said, his voice deep and breathy.

Mortified, Rusty tiptoed back to his room and shut the door. What the heck had he done? The professors had been so kind and gentle with him, and he'd repaid them by spying on an incredibly intimate moment.

He crawled back into bed and pretended not to hear the soft knock on the door or the soft whisper of his name.

Chapter One

Rusty glanced at his iPad to check the time. He'd been sitting on a concrete bench outside the science building for almost thirty minutes, dreading, yet excited to see Professor Ryan again for the first time since the weekend of his attack.

He'd made a fool of himself that weekend. Rusty cringed. He still couldn't believe they'd caught him watching them. It had been innocent at first, but he'd blatantly decided to stay and watch Manuel fuck Adam without a single regard as to their privacy. He'd been so embarrassed, he'd asked to go home the next morning and hadn't spoken to either of them since. It hadn't helped that the dreams of his attack had kept him in a constant state of fear. *We'll be back.* The single phrase continued to torment him to the point that it had been three weeks since he'd left BK House. Chase had tried to help by delivering his class work, but tests all had to be taken in person, and his Ecotoxicology final, taught by Professor Ryan, was in five minutes.

Sadly, his mortification was so great he'd considered blowing off the test. It had been his love and his parents' love for the environment that had pushed him to step foot out of BK House. He wanted to make a difference. He had the brains to make a fortune in a lab somewhere, but money had never meant much to him or his parents. Before his parents' accident, they'd often talked about how man was destroying the planet a piece at a time, and he'd promised them he'd do something about it.

With a sigh, he shouldered his messenger bag and climbed the steps of the science building.

He found his usual spot in the front row of the large lecture hall and stowed his bag on the chair next to him. He didn't need to worry about someone sitting there because they never did, as if they thought his awkwardness was catching.

Rusty leaned his cheek on his hand. Although he was used to feeling like an outcast it still hurt. His spirits lifted a bit when he thought of Chase. His roommate had become a true friend over the last few weeks. It was more than he'd ever had, and he still couldn't believe someone as popular and handsome as Chase wanted anything to do with him, but he accepted the friendship with open arms.

Professor Ryan walked into the room, looking perfectly rumpled in a pair of faded jeans, an Aerosmith T-shirt and the familiar wrinkled white lab coat he usually wore. He brushed his shaggy brown hair out of his face before his gaze landed on Rusty.

Rusty held his breath as he gave his teacher a tentative smile. Professor Ryan smiled in return and with a subtle nod, went back to his preparations. Rusty clung to the simple gesture, hoping it meant the professor didn't regret being so tender with him after the attack, before Rusty had spied on the professors like a darn pervert.

"You'll have two hours to complete the exam," Professor Ryan announced as he handed his teaching assistant Brad a stack of tests to pass out.

Rusty's gaze zeroed in on Professor Ryan's hands. He remembered the way those long, slim fingers had dug into Professor Corto Delgado's back as he'd taken his pleasure.

"Hey," Professor Ryan said, placing his hand on Rusty's shoulder.

Rusty glanced up, afraid he'd made a noise or something and realized everyone was filing out of the lecture hall. "What's going on?"

"Time's up. The test is over." The professor sat in the open seat next to the messenger bag. "I appreciate the gesture of you showing up today, but you have to actually take the test for it to count." He grinned, softening the statement.

Rusty felt his face heat in embarrassment. How did he tell his teacher that he'd spent the last two hours in a fog of lustful thoughts? He scrambled to think of something to excuse his actions. "I had an aunt who I'd never met before try to go against my mom and dad's wishes and have them buried, but I beat her to the punch by having them cremated."

Professor Ryan's dark brown eyebrows furrowed. It was obvious he wasn't prepared for the quick change in conversation, but, like he always had, he tried to show compassion. "And that's what they wanted?"

"Yeah. They believed the planet was too small to take up space after they were gone." Rusty pushed his glasses up on his nose. "I have their ashes back at BK, but I haven't figured out where to spread them."

"Or maybe you're just not ready to say goodbye," Professor Ryan offered. He squeezed Rusty's hand. "How're you doing dealing with the attack?"

Rusty shrugged. "I have nightmares. They said they'd be back, so I keep waiting."

"I think they said that to scare you." He brushed his thumb across the back of Rusty's hand. "Come by the lab later, and I'll let you retake the test."

"You don't have to do that." Rusty could have kicked himself. He'd been invited to the hallowed grounds of Professors Ryan and Corto Delgado, of course he was going to go. "But I'd appreciate it."

"Good." Professor Ryan released Rusty's hand and stood. "I should be finished and back to the lab around five."

"I'll be there. Thank you." Rusty watched Professor Ryan's ass as he walked away, remembering what was under the lab coat. When he felt his face heat again, he decided to get out of there before he made a fool of himself.

* * * *

After a long day of classes, Adam walked into the lab and dropped his bag to the floor.

"Class that bad, *mi cielo*?" Manny asked, without looking up from his work.

Adam moved to stand behind Manny. "Rusty was back today."

"Really?" Manny slid off his stool and turned to face Adam. "How'd he look?"

"As tempting as always with a dash of sorrow and embarrassment thrown into the mix." Adam leaned his head against Manny's shoulder. "I can't tell you how much I wanted to wrap my arms around him."

He still hadn't figured out his obsession with Rusty, but he was grateful Manny didn't condemn him for it. In fact, Manny had concurred with Adam's feelings after the night of the attack. Of course, Manny was also the voice of reason.

"If he wanted us, he could've joined us weeks ago. Instead, he ran away and locked himself in his dorm. I doubt he has much experience, and seeing the two of us like that messed with his head."

"I know," Adam replied, tilting his chin up for a kiss. He'd heard it a hundred times before. Rusty's age and inexperience were definitely problems. "But imagine how soft and pale his skin would be against yours."

"*Dios,*" Manny said. He placed his palms on Adam's ass and squeezed. "Would you watch me fuck him?"

Adam had thought a lot about watching Manny and Rusty together and each time he'd hardened to the point of pain. "Every day, in every position," Adam replied, grinding his hardening cock against Manny.

Manny lowered his head and licked Adam's lips before delving in for a deep kiss. Adam moaned and began to unbutton Manny's white lab coat. When his hand met bare skin, he broke the kiss. Manny had been playing with himself again, which meant he'd been deep in thought. As odd as it sounded, Manny did his best thinking with a hand gently rubbing his shaft. "Hmmm, you've been working hard today."

Manny held the sides of his coat back. The drawstring on the light blue hospital scrub pants he preferred had been loosened and the waistband tucked under his heavy ball sac. "*Si,* and I only got carried away once."

Adam palmed Manny's erection with one hand and cupped his balls with the other. He was on his way down to his knees when there was a knock on the door. "That's Rusty. His mind was elsewhere during the test so I'm going to let him retake it tonight."

Manny brushed Adam's hands away before reaching to pull up his pants.

"No," Adam said, holding Manny's pants down. "Just button your coat. I want to see exactly what Rusty does to you."

Manny grinned and shook his head. "I'm not sure Rusty's ready for something like that."

"I doubt he'll know. He's too shy to openly stare at your groin, and you're covered by the lab coat," Adam argued.

With a resigned sigh, Manny began to button his coat. "If you're not careful, you'll scare him away for good," he warned.

The knock sounded again.

Adam gave Manny a quick kiss before rushing to the door. His own dick was hard behind the fly of his jeans, but as often as Rusty stared at it during class, he was probably used to it. He opened the door and smiled at the way the overhead light in the hall made Rusty's deep red hair shine. God, he wanted to lick every pale freckle on Rusty's innocent-looking face. "Sorry to keep you waiting. We were in the middle of something."

Rusty blushed and pushed his glasses up. "I can come back later if you need me to."

"Don't be silly." Adam stepped back and ushered Rusty into the lab. "Manny's here. I hope you don't mind."

Rusty stuck his hands in his pockets. "Not at all. Good evening, Professor Corto Delgado."

Manny chuckled. "I've told you before, just call me Manny."

Rusty glanced at Manny and nodded before staring at the floor once again. "I'll try."

Although Rusty appeared uncomfortable, he'd already checked out the fly of Adam's jeans twice in the short time he'd been in the lab. "And away from class, you can call me Adam."

The tip of Rusty's pink tongue slipped out to lick his bottom lip. The action almost sent Adam to his knees. The deep groan coming from Manny's side of the room told Adam he wasn't the only one who'd noticed.

"Where would you like me to sit?" Rusty asked, digging two pencils from his messenger bag.

Adam glanced around the combined office and lab space. He caught Manny subtly rubbing his length against the side of the lab table. "We were getting ready to order some pizza for dinner, interested?"

Rusty pushed his glasses up on his nose. "Ummm, yeah, I guess. I mean, if you don't mind sharing, and if I can eat it while I take the test."

Adam's cock began to harden. *Goddamn.* Rusty made him want. Before he could answer, Manny interrupted.

"We don't mind at all. We like to share."

Adam narrowed his eyes at Manny and tried to distract Rusty. He ushered him over to the messy desk and began to clear a space. "Sorry, I don't allow my TA in here to clean up after me, and I'm the worst kind of packrat."

Rusty grinned. "So was my dad."

"Go ahead and make yourself comfortable while I call in the pizza," Adam said as he transferred a stack of papers to a side table.

Rusty bit his bottom lip, and Adam had to wonder whether the guy was teasing him on purpose. "Are you sure I'm not going to bother the two of you?"

Adam fished the test out of his bag before setting it in front of Rusty. From the opposite side of the desk, he leaned over, putting himself even closer to Rusty. He didn't want to scare the younger man, but he'd had a moment of holding Rusty, and he wanted more, a lot more. He ducked his head down to look into Rusty's eyes. "I thought maybe you'd call while you were away."

Rusty blinked. "Why would you want me to do that?" He glanced at Manny. "I never got the nerve to apologize for what happened." He adjusted his glasses in a nervous fashion. "There's no excuse for what I did, and I'm sorry."

Adam cupped Rusty's cheek before he could stop himself. "We weren't embarrassed at all." He brushed his thumb over Rusty's soft lips. "In fact, you had us both so worked up that weekend that I'm surprised you only caught us once." He glanced at Manny. "Isn't that right?"

Manny nodded.

"What're you saying?" Rusty asked.

Adam couldn't take his eyes off that sweet lower lip. Fuck. He wanted to taste Rusty. He pressed his thumb against Rusty's lip again and nearly groaned when Rusty parted for him. He waited, wondering what Rusty would do next. "We want you," Adam confessed.

The tip of Rusty's tongue touched the pad of Adam's thumb before he spoke. "Why would you?"

Adam braced his hands on the desk and leaned closer. "Because we can't stop thinking about you," he whispered against Rusty's lips. He sealed their lips together and touched his tongue against Rusty's.

Rusty reared back before Adam could fully engage in the kiss that he'd thought of so many times. "What're you doing?"

Fuck! Had he just made an ass out of himself? He slowly straightened to his full height. "Sorry," he mumbled. He glanced at the clock on the wall. "You'll have until seven-thirty to complete the test."

Adam retreated to the opposite side of the room, seeking comfort from the man he loved. Manny rested his hand on Adam's lower back and ushered him to the private restroom attached to their lab. "What the fuck did I just do?"

Manny wrapped his arms around Adam and pulled him close. "I told you he's not ready." He kissed Adam's temple. "That said, I don't think he's disgusted by the idea, just scared."

Adam had never been able to explain why he felt a connection to Rusty. For almost four years he'd watched Rusty, hoping the time would come when he could get closer to his student. When Rusty's parents had been killed and Eric, Rusty's roommate at the time, had sought Adam's help to pull Rusty out of the almost-catatonic state he'd fallen into, Adam had thought things between them had changed. When Rusty had left town to deal with his parents' estate, Adam had prayed Rusty would seek him out upon his return, but that hadn't happened. In fact, Rusty had seemed to pull away from him even more. Then the attack had occurred and, once again, Adam had got his hopes up.

Adam leaned forward and rested his cheek on Manny's chest. "Tell me again how much you love me?"

"You are *mi cielo*, of course I love you," Manny whispered.

"I love you too. Always," Adam added. Although they'd been together since grad school, they'd broken up for three years after they'd graduated. Manny's student visa had expired and he'd been forced to return to Barcelona. Adam had dated around after Manny had left, but he'd never forgotten the man who truly owned his heart. It was during that time that Adam had first met the geeky redhead who preferred to sit in the front row of all his classes. He'd been charmed by Rusty immediately, and had come close to asking him out when Manny had called to let him know he'd earned a visiting professor position at the university. Although Adam had been ecstatic with the news, his interest in Rusty hadn't waned. He'd been honest with Manny, but it had taken the death of Rusty's parents for Manny to truly understand why Adam felt the way he did.

"Instead of having the pizza delivered, why don't you run out and pick it up," Manny suggested, kissing Adam's forehead. "I'll see if I can set Rusty at ease while you're gone."

"Don't scare him even more," Adam begged. "God, I feel like we're so close."

"Pizza," Manny reminded Adam.

"Right."

* * * *

After tucking his cock away, Manny went back to his work while Adam told Rusty he was running out for the pizza. Manny watched the pair out of the corner of his eye until Adam left the office.

When Adam had first confessed his attraction to Rusty, Manny had been hurt. He'd given up so much to return to the United States to be with the only man he'd ever loved, and to find out Adam had eyes for someone else had nearly destroyed their relationship, but Manny had refused to walk away. His love for Adam was blinding and for a while, he'd pushed aside his partner's crush. It hadn't been until the night Rusty's parents had been killed that he'd witnessed the obvious connection between Adam and Rusty. Although it had been innocent at the time, watching Adam hold and soothe a distraught Rusty had angered and aroused him, but more than that, it had planted a seed in Manny's mind and heart. There was no denying he'd found Rusty's vulnerability sexy the moment they'd met, but taking care of Rusty after the attack had somehow implanted the younger man in his heart. He'd soon realized that he could no longer deny Adam or himself the chance to get to know Rusty on a sexual and emotional level.

Manny chanced another peek at Rusty. With his pencil hovering over the test, Rusty appeared to be shell-shocked. Mouth open the slightest bit, Rusty hadn't taken his eyes off the door Adam had recently walked through. "Are you okay?"

Rusty blinked several times before peering up at Manny. "Uhhh, yeah." He shook his head before returning his gaze to the paper in front of him.

Manny wasn't sure what to do or say. The caretaker in him wanted to set Rusty's mind at ease, but scaring him was the last thing he wanted. "Have you ever been with two men at the same time?"

Rusty shook his head but didn't look up from the test.

"Does the thought scare you?" Manny continued.

Rusty shrugged and tapped his paper with the point of his pencil. "I need to finish this."

Manny backed off, but he hoped he'd given Rusty something to think about. "I'll leave you to it." He turned his attention to the messy worktable, wishing he had the words to ease Rusty's fears. He busied himself with clearing enough space for dinner, only glancing over his shoulder to check on Rusty a handful of times.

When the door opened and Adam came back into the office, carrying two pizzas, Manny let out a silent sigh of relief. A quick check of the clock told him Rusty still had an hour left. "Can Rusty's test be interrupted long enough to eat?"

Adam set the boxes on the table. "Rusty? Why don't you take a thirty minute break?"

"I'm almost finished," Rusty replied without taking his eyes off his work.

Rusty's statement didn't surprise Manny—he'd heard countless stories of Rusty's brilliance from Adam over the last few years. He opened a cabinet and retrieved three plastic plates before opening the mini-fridge. "Beer?" he asked Rusty as he pulled out two bottles.

"No thank you," Rusty said, setting down his pencil.

Manny handed a beer to Adam as Rusty stood and gathered his test papers.

"Should I leave this here?" Rusty asked.

"Yeah, that's fine," Adam answered.

Manny didn't miss the nervous waiver in Adam's voice. "Come and eat," he said to Rusty, hoping to ease the situation. Unfortunately, the moment he saw Rusty reach for his messenger bag, Manny knew the evening wasn't going to end well.

"Thanks, but I need to go." Rusty settled the strap on his shoulder as he walked to the office door. With his hand on the knob, he glanced back to look at Adam and Manny. "I'm sorry. I need you to know it's not that I'm not attracted to you because I am, but I promised my mom I'd save that part of myself for the right man." He shrugged. His face was red with apparent embarrassment. "I know that sounds corny, and if my mom was still here, I'd probably discuss this with her, but she's not, so I can't go back on a promise I made in good faith."

"Who's to say there's only one right man for you?" Adam asked. He wrapped his arm around Manny's waist. "So you know, we've never invited someone into our bed, and we wouldn't have asked unless it meant something to us."

Rusty shook his head again. "Three people would never work, and I don't think I could survive being dropped when the two of you realize it, too." Without another word, he opened the door and walked out into the hall.

Manny watched the door close behind Rusty and felt the bone deep truth of Rusty's words. He'd feared the same thing, although in his head, it had always been him who Adam dropped. For two years he'd told himself it was irrational, but Adam's interest in Rusty hadn't wavered since the first moment Rusty had walked into Adam's lecture hall.

"I'll change his mind," Adam said, a determined tone to his voice.

Loving Adam more than he loved himself, Manny nodded because whether or not he ended up losing Adam in the process, he also wanted Rusty.

* * * *

Rusty barely remembered the walk back to the dorm or dropping his messenger bag on the floor of his room before crawling into bed. He pulled his laptop off the shelf over the bed and checked his email. When twelve unread messages appeared on the screen, he sighed. They were all from members of his extended family. "Why can't you all just leave me alone?"

He marked each of them as spam before powering off the computer. In all his years growing up, never had he met a single cousin, aunt or uncle, but after his parents' death, they'd seemed to come out of the woodwork, each of them claiming they deserved a share of the estate. His aunt had even gone went as far as saying Rusty's mom had promised her a sizable amount of money before she died.

Rusty knew it was a lie because his mom, Gretta, had had absolutely nothing to do with her family. He was staring at the ceiling when Chase came in.

"Hey," Chase said, dropping onto his old bed. "How'd your first day back go?"

Rusty glanced at his friend. "It was okay. I think I passed my test." Actually, he had no idea whether or not he'd done well. Heck, he barely remembered taking the darn thing. "Why aren't you with Mac?"

Chase shrugged and lay back on a pillow, his hands clasped under his head. "I told him I wanted to hang out with you for a while. I thought maybe I could get you to go to the Burger Barn with me."

Rusty eyed his roommate. Chase was never home on his night off, so the fact he was willing to forgo an evening with Mac to spend it with him was oddly comforting. Still, it had been his first day out of BK House and although nothing had happened, he wasn't comfortable tempting fate. "Why don't we order something in and watch TV?"

Chase groaned. "Come on, man, you're letting that asshole dictate your life. Let's just go out and have a fucking burger."

Rusty groaned. It was an ongoing argument between the two of them. For weeks Chase had tried to get him out of the room, but the thought of his attacker finding him again kept Rusty cowering inside the safe confines of the dorm. Each time he'd tried to venture out, he couldn't help but wonder if each man he passed was his attacker. By the time he'd reached his destination, he'd been reduced to a shaking, paranoid mess. It had taken all his courage to take his tests earlier, and he didn't think he had any left. Besides, he really needed to talk to Chase about Adam and Manuel. He rubbed his face with his hands and shook his head. He couldn't believe he was going to tell someone what had happened, but the situation confused him. It was hard to understand why either man would want him, but more than that, why they would be willing to share each other with someone else.

"What?" Chase asked.

Rusty took a deep breath. "Have you ever...?" He shook his head again. How the heck did he talk about this without prying into Chase's past? "Would you and Mac ever take another man to your bed?"

Chase's eyebrows rose before pulling back down. He frowned and reached for Rusty's hand. "I'm sorry, man, but I don't like you in that way."

Realization dawned on Rusty. "Oh, no, not me with you." He pulled his hand back, breaking contact with Chase. *Dang.* His cheeks burned with mortification at the mistaken come on, but he couldn't stop without making the situation clear. Losing one of his few friends because of a misunderstanding wasn't going to happen. "I think Professor Ryan and Professor Corto Delgado want me to *be* with them."

Chase smiled. "Of course they do. I mean, I knew Professor Ryan was interested in you that night he came here when your parents died. And, after seeing the possessive way Professor Corto Delgado took control when you were attacked, I can see he feels the same."

Rusty groaned and covered his face. "I can't do it."

"Why the hell not? There aren't many gays on this campus that wouldn't jump at the chance to be in the middle of a professor sandwich."

Professor sandwich? "Yeah, that sounds about right. I'll be nothing but a piece of meat to them." That was exactly what worried Rusty. Adam and Manuel were in love. He'd seen it the few times he'd been around them. Sure, they'd invited him in to spice up their sex life, but that didn't mean they'd want anything more, and he wanted the more.

* * * *

Manny gathered Adam into his arms and kissed his temple. It had taken an entire weekend of nonstop loving to prompt the slightest smile from Adam's handsome face. Manny had hoped Rusty would change his mind about their offer, but it had been two weeks. Each day Adam returned from class with Rusty, he seemed more distant. It was still worrisome, despite their continued lovemaking.

"I love you, *mi cielo*," Manny whispered.

"I love you, too," Adam replied. He kissed Manny's collarbone.

Manny bit his lower lip. He'd given the situation a lot of thought, and the only answer he'd come up with would threaten everything he'd built with Adam. "*Mi madrastra* wants me to go home for the holidays."

Adam leaned up on his elbow and stared at Manny. "You're not going, are you?"

Manny shrugged and laid out his plan. "It might be for the best. This will be Rusty's first Thanksgiving and Christmas without his parents. Maybe you can draw him in if I'm not around."

"No. The whole point is for the three of us to be together," Adam argued.

"*Sí*, but the two of us together are overwhelming to him. It might be better to ease him into our lives if we do it one at a time."

"Okay, we'll do that then, but that doesn't mean you have to leave. Let me talk to him first before you decide to leave the country. I'll try to convince him to date us individually. That way we'll both be sure of our feelings for him."

Manny knew jealousy could become a problem, but he doubted it would be any worse than if he were thousands of miles away while Adam pursued Rusty. "We've never been with someone else without each other."

"I know." Adam moved to straddle Manny's groin. He swiveled his hips several times until Manny's cock started to harden once more. "Hopefully, the end result will be worth it. All we have to agree on is whether or not we openly share with each other what goes on while we're with Rusty."

Manny reached down and held his erection by the base as Adam slowly eased it inside. With his shaft buried to the hilt, he rested his hands on Adam's hips. Although he didn't know whether or not he could handle hearing the details of Adam's dates with Rusty, he would no doubt conjure worse things in his mind if he was left in the dark. Still... "I don't know. Why don't we wait and see? Things may not get that far."

Adam braced his hands on Manny's shoulders and started to move. "If it doesn't, it won't be for lack of trying."

Manny closed his eyes and tried to concentrate on the squeeze of Adam's inner muscles around his length. It was the third time in the last twelve hours that he'd buried himself in Adam's ass and each time he did, he couldn't help but lose himself in the sensation. It didn't matter that the usual citrus scent of Adam's cologne had been replaced by the smell of sweat and cum. Adam made love with the sweetest combination of gentleness and savagery. An intoxicating mix that had enslaved Manny's heart since their first time together. He wrapped his arms around Adam's waist and rolled, finding a relatively clean spot on the dove gray sheets Adam preferred. Looking down at Adam's surprised expression, he grinned. "My turn."

Adam licked his lips before pulling Manny down for a deep kiss. "Fuck me," he begged. "Fuck me harder than you ever have."

Manny lapped at Adam's mouth, tasting the Red Bull they'd drunk to refuel earlier. Good thing, too, because it seemed Adam was no longer in the mood to make love. Manny knew it was semantics, but given their earlier conversation about Rusty, the request stung. He sat back on his heels, a move that dislodged his cock from Adam's hole. "On your knees."

Adam quickly complied before glancing over his shoulder. "Make me scream."

"Absolutely." With conflicted emotions, Manny lined up the crown of his erection and plunged deep inside Adam with one powerful thrust of his hips. He stared through the wall of glass at the setting sun as he began to fuck Adam without mercy.

"Christ!"

"Too much?" Manny asked without slowing the pace or intensity of his movements. The slapping of his balls against Adam on each thrust fueled his lust even further.

"Hell no," Adam ground out, his voice barely more than a guttural groan.

Manny dug his fingertips harder into Adam's hips as he slammed in hard. He loved the sounds Adam made—a combination of moans and grunts as their skin slapped together. Hell, he loved every inch of Adam, which made sharing him feel wrong. Manny wanted Rusty as much as Adam did, but how selfish were they to find perfection and continue to look for more?

Manny lowered his head and stared at his dick as it slid in and out of Adam's hole in quick succession. *Fuck.* The way Adam's body accepted Manny's length should be enough for anyone, so why couldn't he get the dream of Rusty bending over for him out of his mind? He shook the thought away and slid one hand down to wrap around Adam's erection. "Tell me why you want him?"

Adam glanced over his shoulder. "You're asking me this now? We can talk about it later. Like, after I come?"

"We'll talk about it now," Manny corrected. He draped his torso over Adam's spine to whisper in his ear. "Am I not enough?"

Ignoring Manny's question, Adam swatted Manny's hand away before pumping himself to completion.

Manny's entire body yearned for climax, but his troubling thoughts kept him from seeking his own release.

Adam sighed and collapsed under Manny's weight. He buried his face in the pale gray sheets and moved it from side to side. "It has nothing to do with whether or not you're enough," he mumbled into the mattress.

Manny withdrew from Adam's body before rolling to the side. After having his cock buried inside Adam, the cool air of the bedroom felt like ice on his failing erection but he paid it no mind as he gathered Adam into his arms. "Talk to me."

"Why? We've talked about this a million times, and it's obvious you still don't want it."

Manny took a deep breath. "I do want it. That's the problem. I can't figure out my own mind, so I'm hoping to understand yours. Why do we need someone else?"

Adam rested his cheek on Manny's chest. "I don't know. We're taught by our parents and society that love should be between two people, that if someone owns your heart, there shouldn't be room for anyone else, but that doesn't make sense to me. I mean, couples have more than one child and don't worry about loving one more than the other because their capacity to love grows with each newborn. Why can't the same be true for a romantic relationship? It's not that you're not enough for me. It's that I also have feelings for someone else, too. That doesn't diminish, in any way, what the two of us have together."

Manny stared at the wall, watching the pink cast of the setting sun slowly fade. Adam was right. He knew because even though his dick hardened every time he thought of Rusty, it hadn't lessened his love for Adam in the least. "Ask him out and see what he says," he finally agreed.

Chapter Two

"Rusty, can I talk to you in my office?" Adam asked after class on Monday.

Rusty slung his messenger bag over his shoulder. He'd known it was only a matter of time before the professor started to regret his actions a few weeks earlier. "Don't worry about it," he said, hoping to put his favorite teacher at ease.

Adam shook his head. "Please. Let's talk in my office."

The last thing Rusty wanted was to be in an enclosed room with his sexy, rumpled professor, but he nodded. "I have another class in an hour."

"Okay." Adam started walking toward the side door, but stopped and turned back. "Are you coming?"

Rusty still wasn't sure. He'd thought about little else since Adam had propositioned him, but he couldn't help but wonder if he would be walking into the lion's den. "Yeah." He followed Adam out of the lecture hall, down the long highway and up two flights of stairs. "Is Professor Corto Delgado here?"

"No. Manny's in Eugene at the University of Oregon conferring with a colleague." Adam unlocked the office and gestured for Rusty to precede him. "He'll be back late tonight."

Searching for something to say, Rusty let his messenger bag fall off his shoulder as he sat in front of Adam's desk. "Does he travel often?"

Adam shrugged. He opened a small refrigerator and withdrew two bottles of water. "Not often, a day or two each month, but he's rarely gone overnight." He handed a bottle to Rusty. "I need to apologize for the way I came onto you."

"I told you, don't worry about it." Rusty took a drink. He sat on the front edge of the cushion, ready to bolt if necessary. As uncomfortable as he'd thought the meeting would be, it was worse. He swallowed the water and silently cursed his body's reaction to the handsome man standing over him. *Dang.* When his cock started to harden, he knew he had to get out of there. "Is that all?" he asked, getting to his feet.

Adam sat on the corner of the desk and placed his hand on Rusty's shoulder. "Sit. I want to explain myself."

"Really, Professor, there's no need." Rusty stared at the hand on his shoulder and waited for Adam to remove it. Although Adam was smaller than Manny, he was still a lot bigger than Rusty, which made the differences between Rusty and Manny ridiculous.

"I want you to go out with me on a real date. I want you to see that we could be good together."

"Why? You've already got someone in your life." A thought struck Rusty. "Are the two of you not getting along?"

"Manny and I are better than ever. That's what I need you to understand. Our interest in you is entirely mutual. I just think it would be easier for you to understand if you got to know us better one on one."

It didn't make sense. Manny and Adam were incredibly hot men, so why in the world would they be interested in dating someone who definitely didn't even rank on the stud scale? And why the heck would they be willing to go through the hassle of dating him in the first place? Rusty threw up his hands. "To what end? What's the point? I'm not interested in being your little sex toy. I know I may not show it, but I do have feelings and they can be hurt."

Adam's features softened. "We're not trying to hurt you. We want to love you."

Why in the heck would two people who are already devoted to each other want to love someone else? The worst part about the situation was that he knew he'd be the one to develop feelings first. He yearned to love someone who wasn't dead, which was a really crappy way of looking at it, but it was the truth. He wanted to love and be loved, but what if giving into his desires for the two men only led to him being hurt? "What happens if only one of you falls in love with me or if I fall in love with Manny and not you?" He shook his head vehemently. "I won't put myself into a love triangle when I know they never work."

"That's why we think it's important to date. You and I can get to know each other better while you and Manny do the same. We'll take things slowly at first if that's what you need. We're asking for a chance to build something special, but it'll take a leap of faith on your part."

Rusty took off his glasses and cleaned them with the tail of his untucked plaid shirt. Since the moment he'd walked into Adam's class, he'd been attracted to the handsome professor. His interest in Adam had gone beyond the faded jeans and old band T-shirts. Adam's messy hair gave him that just-rolled-out-of-bed look that Rusty had always found fantasy-worthy, but never in a million years had he thought he'd actually have a chance with him. Adding Manny into the mix only made the prospect even more unbelievable because Manny's chiseled facial features and muscular build made him romance-cover material. "Can I think about it?"

Adam's tentative smile fell at the question. "Sure."

Rusty grabbed his bag off the floor. As much as he was dying to agree to the arrangement, he always felt better about his decisions when he took the time to dissect them and look at all consequences. "I'll call you."

Adam grinned. "You still have my number?"

"Of course," Rusty said before he could think better of it.

"That has to be a sign or something, right?"

Rusty opened the office door. *Was it?* "Maybe," he replied before shutting the door behind him. He readjusted his bag on his shoulder and headed toward the dorm. He needed to talk to someone, but Chase was working the evening shift at the bar, so he called Eric.

"Hey, what's up?" Eric answered.

"Are you busy?" Rusty stopped at one of the stone benches in the quad and sat.

"Not really. Just watching Will cook dinner. Why? Is something going on?"

Rusty knew from his own childhood how important dinnertime was to a family, even if that family only consisted of two. "No problem. I thought we could catch up, but that's okay."

"Don't be stupid. Come over and eat with us. Will's making sloppy joes and fried potatoes."

Rusty's stomach grumbled at the mention of one of his favorite meals. His mom had never liked to cook, so most dinners had been quick and easy. "I'd like that," he admitted.

"Cool. See you in a bit."

Rusty hung up and shoved the phone into his pocket. Instead of running home to get his car, he considered hopping on a bus, but decided against it. Although he was slowly starting to get out more, he knew he'd feel safer in his own vehicle, and with his mind on Adam's proposition, he doubted he'd stay vigilant on the ride to Will's house.

Decision made, he walked as fast as he could across the campus, between the regular dorms, to the back of BK House. He waved to the older woman who lived next door to the dorm. "Good evening, Mrs Fisher."

Ida Fisher neared the fence that separated the two properties, beckoning Rusty. He hated to be mean to the lonely woman, so he walked several steps toward her.

"Would you like to earn some money?" Ida asked.

Rusty smothered a grin. "Do you need help with something?"

Ida nodded and pointed to her gutters. "I asked my grandson to help me clean them, but he said it might be another few weeks before he gets to them. Well, I was watching the news earlier and they're expecting rain this week. I thought maybe I'd offer to pay you a couple of dollars, and you could take care of them for me."

Rusty had never cleaned a gutter, let alone been up a ladder, but he couldn't say no to the sweet lady. "Can it wait until tomorrow? I don't have a class until ten, so I can do it first thing in the morning." He had no idea how to do it, but surely it wouldn't be that difficult.

Ida's expression brightened. "You're such a good boy. I told my grandson that I was going to ask you, but he said I should wait for him."

"That's okay, Mrs Fisher. I'll do it." He smiled and lifted his hand, hoping to get away without more friendly chatter. "I'm going to a friend's for dinner, but I'll knock on your door in the morning. Do you have a ladder?"

"Yes. One of those good sturdy wooden ones. It belonged to Howard," she added.

Mrs Fisher was nearly eighty, and Rusty knew from talking with her before that Howard had been twelve years older than she was. He worried about the condition of the ladder, but nodded in acknowledgment. "Good. See you tomorrow."

Rusty slipped away before she could say anything else. As much as he cared for the elderly woman, she couldn't help him with his current predicament, but he hoped Eric could.

* * * *

"So what's up?" Eric asked as he piled fried potatoes onto his plate.

Like with Chase, Rusty wasn't sure how to start the conversation. "I got asked out on a date," he declared.

"That's fantastic," Eric replied. "Do I know him?"

Rusty stared down at his dinner. "Professor Ryan." He cleared his throat. "Actually, Professor Ryan and Professor Corto Delgado want to go out with me. Separately, at first, but they're hoping for something more."

When his answer was met by silence, Rusty glanced up. If their gaping mouths were any indication, Will and Eric appeared surprised by the news. Rusty shifted in his chair. "It's crazy, right? They're going to use me, aren't they?"

With a slight shake of his head, Will lowered the bite of food he had loaded onto his fork. "I don't think you can assume they're going to use you, but it is risky. It's hard enough to make a relationship work with one man—two?" He sighed. "It would take an incredibly strong bond between the three of you. Will it be hard work? Absolutely. But I know Adam and Manny, and I doubt they've taken the decision to approach you lightly."

"I didn't know they were friends of yours," Rusty replied, looking from Will to Eric.

"We've had dinner with them several times since..." Eric bit his bottom lip. "Since the night your parents died." He held up his hands. "Don't worry though, other than asking how you were doing, they didn't try to get any of your secrets out of me."

"That wouldn't have been hard since I don't have any secrets." Rusty inwardly winced at the white lie.

Eric's features softened as he leaned his forearms on the small table, putting himself closer to Rusty. "I know about your parents. I saw some papers on your desk. I didn't say anything because I knew I wasn't supposed to see them."

Rusty glanced at Will, wondering if he also knew.

"No. I haven't said anything to anyone," Eric said as if reading Rusty's mind. "If Adam and Manny want you, it's for you and not your money."

Rusty released the breath he'd been holding. His mom and dad had always warned him about men who would try to take advantage of him if they knew how much he was worth. He hadn't thought Adam or Manny were the money-hungry-type, so that hadn't been a consideration. Even so, Eric's assurance made him feel better.

"What?" Will asked, breaking the silence a few moments later.

"I have money," Rusty confessed. "A lot of it. My father liked to tinker in the garage. He patented quite a few inventions that helped clean and protect the environment, most of which were purchased for a great deal of money. Despite her thrifty lifestyle, Mom was a genius when it came to investing. They used a lot of the money to buy land, hoping they could preserve endangered species of wildlife." He shrugged. "But, despite how much they still had invested and in the bank, the house I cleaned out and sold after their deaths was the same home I grew up in, the same one my mom and dad purchased when they had nothing."

"That's probably why you seem so grounded," Eric said.

"Grounded or boring?" Rusty grinned. When they'd roomed together, Eric had always accused Rusty of being a boring nerd. Eric had been right, of course, but Rusty couldn't help but tease his friend.

"Both." Eric chuckled. He picked up his sloppy joe. "So back to Adam's offer. I've known for a while that you're attracted to him, but what about Manny?"

An unbidden image of Manny fucking Adam against the window popped into Rusty's mind. "I like him," he mumbled, thankful the table shielded his hardening cock from view. "I mean, I don't feel like I know him as well as Adam, but I guess that's what the dating is supposed to accomplish."

Eric tried to hide his grin behind his sandwich. "Yeah, he's hot, that's for sure."

Will cleared his throat, and Eric let loose a laugh. "Deny it," Eric said, staring at his partner.

"Can't," Will grumbled, "but, that doesn't mean I need to hear you say it."

After leaning over to give Will a quick kiss, Eric returned his attention to Rusty. "I think you should do it."

"What if I get hurt?" Rusty asked.

"Then you do, but it doesn't matter if you're dating one man or two, the possibility of getting your heart broken is always there when you put yourself out there. Better to take the chance than to always wonder, right?"

"Guess so." Rusty thought of the love his parents had shared. Had they been worried about getting hurt when they'd started dating? He imagined so. "I'll call after dinner."

Eric frowned. "Call now. I'll nuke your food once you're done."

Rusty should have politely declined. It was rude to get up from the table before the meal was finished, but before he could stop himself, he was getting to his feet. He withdrew his phone and gave his friends an apologetic smile. "I'll be right back."

Eric gave him a thumbs-up. "Go for it."

Rusty wandered into the living room, his thumb hovering over Adam's saved number. Never had he been so at odds with himself, but he knew his fear was born of want, and he *wanted* Adam and Manny. *You can do this.* He took a deep breath and hit Adam's name on his display.

"You called," Adam answered, sounding almost... relieved.

"Umm, yeah, I said I would," Rusty replied. He pushed his glasses up higher on his nose. It was a nervous gesture, one he'd adopted after his first run-in with a bully who'd knocked his glasses off his face. The action didn't make sense, even to him, because his glasses were always the first thing a bully went for.

"I know, but I thought I might've scared you off again."

"You didn't." Rusty tapped on the glass, getting the attention of a squirrel raiding Will's birdfeeder. He grinned at the dirty look the squirrel gave him.

"Will you go out with us?" Adam asked, pulling the answer from Rusty.

"Yes, but I need you to promise me that this isn't a game for you. I only have one heart and it's been through enough lately," Rusty confessed.

"Can I see you tonight?"

Rusty glanced toward the dining room. As much as he wanted to see Adam, it would be rude to leave. "I can't. I'm at Will's having dinner."

"Shit. Let me call you right back," Adam said before hanging up.

Rusty stared at his phone. He wondered if Manny had arrived home from his trip, and Adam didn't want Manny to know he'd been making plans to see Rusty? He waited several minutes before pocketing his phone. He was entering the dining room when his cell rang. *Jeez.* He retrieved his phone. "Hello?"

"Please don't be mad, but I texted Will, and he said it was fine for me to come over," Adam said without preamble. "I'll be there in ten minutes."

Rusty stared open-mouthed at his grinning friends. "Ummm, okay."

"Should I bring some beer or a bottle of wine?" Adam asked.

"I don't really drink, but I've had wine before," Rusty admitted. He didn't want Adam to know what a nerd he was. It was one thing to be smart, but Rusty knew most intelligent people also socialized. Unfortunately, other than the odd dinner with Will and Eric or Chase and Mac, he didn't know how to let loose and have fun.

"We've got a few bottles here. I'll bring something you'll like."

"Sounds good." Rusty eased into his chair and ignored his friends. "See you in a bit." He ended the call. "Sorry about that."

"Why? You want to see him, we like him, he's coming over. End of discussion," Will replied.

"I'll build a fire out in the pit, and we can sit out there." Eric got to his feet and picked up his empty plate before disappearing into the kitchen.

Left alone with Will, Rusty stared down at his plate of cold food. He could ask Eric to heat it up, but he was too nervous to eat anyway. He glanced at Will. "I've never dated. I don't really know what I'm supposed to do."

Will scraped the last of the fried potatoes onto his plate. "Do what you feel like doing. There aren't any rules to speak of as long as you're all agreeable. If you want to kiss, kiss. If you want to fuck on the first date, fuck." He grinned. "As long as you go somewhere else if fucking's on the agenda."

Rusty didn't dare admit that he'd never kissed a man. What if he did it wrong? His stomach cramped at the thought of Adam or Manny fucking him. He felt sweat begin to bead on his forehead as visions of naked bodies swam through his mind. His breathing became labored as he fought to push back the images. "Excuse me." He rose and hurried to the small half-bath.

Safely locked inside, Rusty tore off his glasses and bent over the sink to splash his face with cold water.

He needed to get himself together before Adam showed up. He shook his hands in an attempt to rid himself of the anxiety that threatened to overwhelm him. Staring into the mirror, he resettled his glasses. *This is your chance. Don't mess it up.*

* * * *

Legs crossed with his ankle resting on his knee, Adam tried to pay attention to Will, who was telling another story. Usually, he enjoyed Will's amusing tales of life as a detective, but at the moment, Adam couldn't keep his gaze off Rusty.

Each time Rusty took a drink of the cabernet, he smacked his lips. It was the cutest damn thing Adam had ever witnessed, and it was taking all his willpower not to lean over and taste the sweetness of the wine on Rusty's tongue. Adam retrieved the bottle from the table. "Would you like more?"

Rusty bit his bottom lip as he studied his nearly-empty glass. "Just a little. I have to get up early and clean Mrs Fisher's gutters."

"Mrs Fisher? That old lady that lives next door to BK?" Eric asked. He was reclined on a chaise lounge beside Will while Rusty and Adam sat in chairs across from them.

"She's nice," Rusty said defensively. "She's lonely, and she asked me to help her with her gutters."

Eric held up his hands. "Fine. I just don't understand why she'd ask *you*."

Rusty's expression fell as he set his wine glass on the table. "I may not be as strong as everyone else, but I can clean a fucking gutter for a nice lady."

Adam was surprised by Rusty's use of profanity. Never, in the years he'd known him, had Rusty uttered anything more than the tamest of curse words.

"Thanks for dinner, Will, but I need to go," Rusty said as he stood.

"I didn't mean it like that," Eric argued. "I know for a fact Mrs Fisher has a huge family, so why aren't they helping her out?"

Rusty sighed and shook his head slowly from side to side. "I don't know. She said one of her grandsons said he could get to it in a couple of weeks, but she's afraid it'll start raining." He shrugged and the simple movement drew Adam's attention to Rusty's thin, frail shoulders.

"It's nice of you to help her." Adam set his glass beside Rusty's. "You ready?"

"You don't have to go," Eric said, getting to his feet. "I'm sorry if I made you mad."

"It's okay. I'm not mad, but it's getting late, and I still have some homework to do. Talk to you tomorrow, Eric."

"Come on, I'll drive you home," Adam offered, hoping to get a few minutes alone with Rusty. "Thanks for letting me crash your evening," he told Will and Eric.

"I can't leave my car here," Rusty protested.

"You've had several glasses of wine. I'll see that your ride gets back to you tomorrow." Adam rested his hand on Rusty's lower back as they walked through the house and out of the front door. He'd been dying all night to touch and he couldn't deny himself any longer.

"Wow. Is that yours?" Rusty asked, pointing to Adam's Jeep Wrangler.

Adam studied the Jeep. Although it was only two years old, his poor baby was starting to look rather shabby. "I like to take it off-road." He ran his finger over a long scratch in the black paint. "I should probably take better care of her, but she's a wild one and it's hard to keep her from searching for adventure."

Rusty leaned against the passenger door and stared up at Adam. "Is that what you're doing with me? Looking for an adventure?"

Adam moved closer, sandwiching Rusty between his body and the vehicle. He rested his hands on Rusty's trim hips and shook his head. "No." He knew telling Rusty the truth was probably a bad idea, but he needed to be honest. "You have no idea how many men have offered to join me and Manny in bed."

Rusty winced, and Adam quickly continued, "But, you're the only one we've ever invited in." Adam slid his hands up to cup Rusty's face. "I don't know how to make you understand that this isn't just about sex for us."

"That's probably a good thing since I know practically nothing about sex."

The illumination of the street light nearby made it easy for Adam to see the blush creeping up Rusty's neck at the admission. Adam brushed his thumb across Rusty's lower lip. He'd had a feeling Rusty was a virgin, but he needed to find out the full extent of Rusty's experience. "Have you ever been kissed?"

A shake of his head was the only answer Rusty gave Adam. *Fuck.* Adam closed his eyes and took a deep breath. He needed to get his lust under control before he scared Rusty away. "Can I kiss you?"

Although his body stiffened, Rusty dipped his chin in a subtle nod.

Adam tilted Rusty's head back. "Relax," he whispered before pressing their mouths together. He started with soft kisses, progressing slowly until he felt Rusty's lips part in silent invitation. The combination of innocence and passion sent a bolt of pure pleasure racing through Adam as he pressed his erection against Rusty's lean body. *Christ.* He wanted all of the man in his arms, but, after several swipes of his tongue against Rusty's, he pulled back. "Tell me you're lying about never being kissed before because, damn, you're good at it."

Rusty licked Adam's chin before peppering kisses down the column of Adam's throat. "You're my first." He licked Adam's jaw. "I like the feel of your whiskers against my tongue."

Adam's hands started to shake as he fought to keep his control. "Don't say things like that," he murmured. "I'm struggling as it is. God, Rusty, I've never carried someone to my bed, but you're making it really hard to keep myself from doing just that."

"I thought we were dating. Kissing's allowed on dates, right?" Rusty asked.

The confused expression on Rusty's face melted Adam's heart. "Yeah, baby, kissing's allowed, but I doubt it'll ever be enough for me, so I need you to tell me if I try to go further than you're comfortable with." He took a step back. "Let's get you home."

"Will you kiss me goodnight once we get there?"

Adam leaned in and gave Rusty another quick kiss. "If that's what you want. Like I told you, you're going to have to set the pace for us because I want things from you that I know you're not ready for." He opened the passenger door and waited for Rusty to climb in. He cursed himself for believing he could control himself enough to go on innocent dates with a man he had become obsessed with over the years.

"I really liked kissing you," Rusty said when they were almost to BK. "And for a moment, I wanted you to touch me."

Adam groaned and gripped the steering wheel more tightly. Although Rusty's honesty was admirable, it sure as hell wasn't making the situation easier. "Yeah, but I want to do more than touch you," he warned.

"Do you think Manny will want to kiss me when we go out?"

Adam glanced at Rusty. Manny would eat Rusty alive given the chance. "No doubt about it, but you need to set boundaries with him and be firm about them."

"I don't want to make him mad," Rusty replied.

"You won't. Manny's a gentle giant most of the time, but he's got that fiery Spanish blood running through his veins. Believe me, he's not an easy man to say no to, but it'll crush him if he goes too far and scares you away." Adam turned into the BK lot and parked in one of the guest spots. He opened his door, knowing if he kissed Rusty again inside the dark confines of the Jeep, he'd end up trying to convince Rusty to go back to the apartment with him.

Rusty slid out of the Jeep. "Can I call you tomorrow?" he asked when he joined Adam on the sidewalk.

"You can call me anytime you like, but I thought I'd come over in the morning before my hike and help you clean out those gutters." Adam slung his arm over Rusty's shoulders and pulled him close as they walked up the steps to the front door.

"You hike?"

"I don't have classes on Mondays or Thursdays, so I try to get a good hike in before I start work in the lab." Adam gestured to the small bench at one end of the porch. "You want to sit for a minute?"

"Sure." Rusty settled next to Adam. "Does Manny go with you?"

Adam shook his head. "Occasionally, but he doesn't really like it. I think he goes just to shut me up." He grinned. "Do you hike?"

"Only with my parents. They were really into it. They took me to Scotland to walk the West Highland Way for my sixteenth birthday. We went to Peru when I graduated high school."

"I'm jealous." Adam squeezed Rusty's hand. "If we can get those gutters clean early enough for you to go with me, would you?"

"Yeah. I don't have my good boots here, but if we're not going far, I can wear my sneakers." Rusty repositioned himself until he was sitting on one of his legs. "Can I have that kiss now?"

Adam chuckled. "Have I created a monster?"

"I think so because I want to feel your tongue in my mouth again."

"Words like that will get you into trouble," Adam said before kissing Rusty. Unlike earlier, there was nothing innocent about the way Rusty accepted Adam's tongue.

Without breaking their kiss, Rusty straddled Adam and sat in Adam's lap. Groaning, Adam thrust his tongue deeper as he maneuvered Rusty's ass to ride against the rigid length of his cock.

Rusty began to move, grinding his own erection against Adam's stomach.

It was too much and not enough. Adam pulled out of the kiss and stilled Rusty's hips. "Stop," he panted. "Fuck, you're going to make me come."

"I've never felt like this," Rusty admitted, readjusting his glasses. "I don't know what you're doing to me, but you touch me, and I can't seem to get close enough."

"Yeah. I know the feeling." Adam lifted Rusty off his lap. "I need to go before I say to hell with the consequences and fuck you right here."

Rusty stepped back. "Yeah, I need to study anyway." He ran his tongue over his swollen lower lip. "See you in the morning?"

Adam stood and readjusted his erection before shoving his hands in his front pockets. "I'll be here at eight."

"Okay." Rusty pointed to the small yellow and white house next door. "I'll probably be over there somewhere."

Adam kissed Rusty's forehead. "See ya then."

Chapter Three

Rusty watched the passing scenery with enthusiasm. "It's so beautiful out here." He hadn't expected his first date with Manny to be a drive in the country, but he wasn't about to complain.

"*Sí, es hermoso,*" Manny agreed. He gestured over his shoulder to the plastic box in the back seat. "I have to gather more samples, and I thought it would be a good way for us to share something we are both interested in."

"Samples of what?" Rusty asked.

"There's a lake that was once polluted. A dumping ground for people's trash. I have been working to clean it up." Manny glanced at Rusty. "It still is not ready for fish to be re-introduced, but I have hope."

After the morning spent hiking and working on Mrs Fisher's house with Adam, Rusty felt more at ease with the prospect of dating the two men. He'd taken a leap of faith with Adam and so far, it was turning out better than he'd thought possible, but Manny was different. Sexually, he was even more attracted to the hot Spaniard, but he also knew Manny was out of his league. Adam, with his easy-going nature and ready smile, reminded Rusty of his parents, but Rusty knew one kiss from Manny and he was likely to explode.

"I hope it is okay that I brought you here instead of a restaurant," Manny said.

"More than okay." Rusty reached over and laid his hand on Manny's thigh. "My parents would approve of what you're doing. Their whole life was devoted to saving the environment."

"*Sí*, Adam told me. You must be proud."

Rusty withdrew his hand and nodded. "I am. They were good people, but even better parents." He rested his head against the back of the seat and turned his attention to the view out of the passenger window. He wondered if there would ever come a time when thinking about his mom and dad didn't hurt. "I miss them."

"I lost *mi mamá* when I was at university. *Mi padre* remarried soon after. It is the reason I am here and not there. It is hard to see another woman in *mi mamá's* kitchen."

"I can understand that."

"Can you? Because *mi familia* does not. They believe I should be helping with the winery."

Rusty turned his head to gaze at Manny. "Your family owns a winery?" He imagined Manny strolling through the rows of vines heavy with grapes and smiled. "Have you ever stomped the grapes?"

Manny laughed. "Only at parties, and it is not as much fun as it looks." He turned off the gravel road onto a dirt trail. "We will walk from here."

Rusty climbed out of the car and looked up at the dark storm clouds overhead. "Do you think we'll have time for a picnic before it rains?"

Manny shrugged before retrieving the sample box from the back seat. "I have made other arrangements for our picnic." He pointed to a narrow dirt path. "That way." He shifted the box to his left hand before reaching for Rusty's hand with the right. "Do you mind?"

Rusty glanced down at their joined hands. His appeared to be so small compared to Manny's. "It's nice." He willed his body to behave at the innocent contact. "I think Mrs Fisher wants to adopt Adam. Did he tell you how many projects she found for us to do?"

Manny grinned. "No, but he said he needed to go back to take care of something else for her."

"To be honest, I think she's just lonely and searching for an excuse to have us over again. I've always tried to be friendly when I see her outside, but now I think I should probably check on her more often."

Manny lifted Rusty's hand and kissed it without breaking his hold. "You are a kind man."

"Not really. I mean, for a long time, I didn't have any friends here. I think I needed to talk to her as much as she needed me." Rusty hated to admit to Manny what a loser he'd always been in the eyes of others, but the date was all about getting to know one another. "People didn't like me growing up. I guess they could tell I was different and that made me an easy target."

"How long have you known you were gay?" Manny asked.

"I don't know. I mean, it wasn't something I decided, it always was. Doesn't matter though because kids picked on me before any of us even knew what being gay meant."

"So what do you think was so different about you? Your intelligence?"

"Maybe. I've never played sports, not because I don't like the activity, but I've never understood why it was important to prove one person or team was better than the other. And, I suppose my parents had something to do with it." Rusty smiled at the memories flashing through his mind. "My mom recycled before it became the *in* thing to do. She prided herself on reusing and repurposing everything she could — including clothes. I think I was in high school before I received a shirt that hadn't been either pieced together or worn by a stranger before I got it." He didn't add that although he loved his mom with all his heart, he'd often blamed her when people bullied him. In the beginning, he'd understood the need to be thrifty because his dad hadn't made much money, but once their bank account had started to grow, it would have been nice to wear the same kind of clothes the other kids wore.

Manny released Rusty's hand as they stopped in a clearing. "There she is," he said, indicating the small lake. "The first time I came here, there were black trash bags full of garbage everywhere along with old appliances, tires and a few barrels of used motor oil. It was disgusting."

Rusty studied the landscape before his gaze settled on the posted warning sign. "It's gorgeous. You'd never know from looking at it that there's anything wrong with the water."

"That is a blessing and a curse. I've spent almost two years skimming oil from the water with pads, taking away the garbage, replenishing the soil and replanting grass. The water is another matter. I am afraid it will take time to undo the damage done to it."

"Who owns this?" Rusty asked.

"I do. I received a call from the original owner, asking if there was a quick way to clean up a polluted lake. When I came out to assess it, I fell in love with the land. It was obvious after our discussion that the owner did not want to put in the time or money required to do the job correctly, so I bought it from him."

"What'll you do with it afterward?"

"I do not know. Maybe sell it. The important thing was to undo the damage caused by careless people," Manny replied.

"Sell it to me. The Bonham Wildlife Foundation can keep it safe for years to come." Rusty hadn't added to the Foundation's holdings since his parents' death. "It's time I continue my mom and dad's legacy."

"I'll think about it."

* * * *

Manny parked in front of the campus planetarium. "This is better than eating with the bugs, no?"

Rusty grinned. "How'd you know this is one of my favorite places?"

"Because it is every scientist's favorite place." Manny retrieved the blanket and picnic basket from the back seat. So far, their date had gone perfectly. Although, he'd found working alongside Rusty to be enjoyable but frustrating. He'd been tempted to pull Rusty into his arms several times over the last few hours, and he knew it wouldn't get easier once they were in the darkened space.

Manny held the door open for Rusty. He set down the basket and blanket. "We should remove our shoes," he suggested as he pulled off his rubber boots while Rusty did the same. He set both pairs to the side of the door before retrieving their dinner supplies. They walked through the lobby to the main theater. "Walter!" he called out. It had cost him a favor and hefty fee to reserve the entire planetarium for an evening, but he knew he would only get one shot at a first date with Rusty.

"I was starting to believe you'd changed your mind," Walter said, appearing from the attached control room.

"The rain hampered our specimen retrieval, but we finished," Manny explained.

"Well, it's all set." Walter handed Manny a small remote control. "You know how to run the equipment, right?"

"*Sí.*" Manny pocketed the remote for the time being.

"Make sure the doors are all securely shut when you leave. If Adam decides to join you, you'll have to let him in."

Manny nodded in acknowledgment. He had no immediate plans to invite Adam, but he wouldn't rule it out either. "Thank you for this."

Walter waved his hand. "We usually only get a couple people a night through here anyway. This way, I get to go home and have dinner with my wife for a change."

Manny waited for Walter to leave before spreading the blanket in the center of the room. "I hope you like sandwiches." He sat cross-legged on the blanket and began to unload the basket. He pulled out two long hoagies, two bags of potato chips, a container of pasta salad and two bottles of water. He had also stopped at the bakery and purchased frosted brownies, but he would save those for later.

Rusty began to unwrap one of the sandwiches. "Can I ask you something?"

"*Sí*," Manny replied. He took the lid off the salad and placed two forks beside it.

"Why haven't you tried to kiss me?" Rusty asked.

Manny's heart skipped a beat. "Adam warned me to go slow."

Rusty set his dinner aside before crawling on his hands and knees toward Manny. "I may be inexperienced, but I'm not afraid."

Manny's gaze zeroed in on Rusty's perfect mouth. It wasn't the first time his attention had been captured by the light brown freckle in the center of Rusty's lower lip. Before he gave in to his desires, he reached into his pocket and removed the remote. The lights slowly dimmed as the entire curved ceiling came alive with stars.

"I think it's a good thing our food is already cold," Rusty said before pushing the food to the corner of the blanket.

"Why is that?" Manny teased as he wrapped his arm around Rusty's waist and pulled him into his lap.

Rusty dragged his fingers through Manny's hair. "Because dinner is not what I'm hungry for at the moment."

Manny palmed Rusty's ass and squeezed. "Tell me what you want, *mi amor*, and it is yours."

Rusty licked his lips. "Really?"

"*Sí*." Manny waited with bated breath for Rusty to answer.

"I want to kiss you and touch you." Rusty ran his hand down Manny's chest. "And see you."

Manny wasn't sure what to do. He knew it would hurt Adam if he fucked Rusty on the first date, but he didn't think he could undress and *not* fuck him.

"I'm sorry." Rusty scooted off Manny's lap. "It's too early, isn't it?"

"No." Manny reached for Rusty and pulled him back in. "*Mi polla está en la necesidad de su cuerpo,*" he whispered in Rusty's ear.

Rusty gasped. "Your cock needs to feel me?"

"*Sí, mucho,* but Adam," Manny tried to explain.

"You think we should call him?" Rusty asked. He started to unbutton Manny's shirt.

Usually English came easily to Manny, but just then he struggled to find the words. "Not yet." He watched as Rusty ran his hands up and down Manny's exposed chest. Confused couldn't begin to describe his feelings. How had Rusty gone from a shy virgin to the sexual creature in front of him in less than a day?

Rusty pushed Manny's shirt off his shoulders. "You're stunning."

Manny was proud of his body and wasn't the least bit shy about showing it off. "Now your shirt."

Rusty's brow furrowed as he removed his hands from Manny. He crossed his arms over his chest. "You don't want to see my chest."

"I do." It was obvious to Manny that Rusty was either shy or insecure, and he knew things between them could never progress unless Rusty accepted his own body. "Why do you say that? Because your chest is not like mine?"

"Yeah. That, and I'm pale as a ghost with freckles everywhere." Rusty seemed to close in on himself right before Manny's eyes. "There's nothing sexy about me."

"Oh, *bebé.* You are wrong." Manny eased Rusty's T-shirt up, slowly revealing the creamy white skin that he'd been fantasizing about since holding him in his arms after the attack. "Let me see you, and I will prove how perfect you are."

"I guess I should be thankful it's dark in here," Rusty said as Manny removed his shirt.

Manny didn't correct Rusty, but in the overhead glow of the stars, Rusty's skin appeared as bright as the moon. It was breathtaking. He pressed his palm against Rusty's sternum. "I see the difference in our coloring—yours white like an angel, and mine dark like the devil trying to tempt you."

"You're being kind," Rusty muttered.

"No." Manny ran his hand down Rusty's chest. "Feel how hard I am for you."

Rusty's gaze went to the front of Manny's jeans.

"Do you want to touch me?" Manny reached for Rusty's hand, and when Rusty didn't protest, he ran it across his cock. "You did that to me." He released Rusty and was pleased when Rusty didn't pull away. "That should be all the proof you need as to whether or not I find you sexy."

"Would you do me a favor and call Adam to see if he'd like to meet us here?" Rusty asked.

While part of Manny wanted to be selfish with Rusty and refuse to invite Adam into their date, he knew it would be for the best when Rusty started to unzip his jeans. "Do I need to ask Adam to bring lube and condoms?"

"Do we need them?" Rusty sat back on his butt and kicked out of his jeans.

Manny's gaze strayed to the tented plaid boxers. He didn't want to admit that Adam had purchased a large package weeks ago in the hope that Rusty would soon join them. "Well, it is normally the way things are handled when fucking someone new."

"But I'm a virgin. Heck, I had my first kiss last night. I don't think you guys can catch anything from me, and I assume you're both healthy."

"We are," Manny confirmed, "but you should never assume that."

"Okay, but you are, right?"

"*Sí.*" Manny reached down and adjusted his throbbing cock. He pulled out his phone and called Adam.

"Hey, how's it going?" Adam asked.

Manny decided to test Rusty. He unbuttoned his jeans and gestured for Rusty to unzip him. "I need you to grab the lube and meet us at the planetarium. When you get here, call and one of us will let you in."

The television on Adam's end shut off. "What? Dammit, Manny! I told you to take it slow."

Manny watched as Rusty lowered his zipper.

"Are you listening to me?" Adam asked.

Manny heard a drawer slam shut in the background. "Get the good stuff." He got to his feet, putting his open fly at eye level for Rusty.

"You're in so much trouble," Adam huffed.

"You have no idea." Manny stared down at Rusty. "Touch me," he urged.

"Shit!" Adam cursed. "It'll take me about ten minutes to get there."

When Rusty made no move to go any further, Manny decided to take control of the situation. "I'll put you on speaker." He dropped the phone to the blanket before pushing the waistband of his underwear low enough to expose his erection.

Rusty's eyes rounded as he licked his lips. "You're big."

"What's going on?" Adam asked.

Rusty blinked several times before glancing down at the phone. "Adam?"

"Yeah. I'm on my way," Adam replied.

"I don't know what to do." Rusty started to reach for Manny's cock, but stopped and dropped his hands at the last moment. He stared up at Manny. "What happens if I touch you?"

"I'll come," Manny answered honestly.

"Don't scare him!" Adam yelled. "Rusty? Go to the front door and wait for me. I'm almost there."

Manny ground his teeth together. It was obvious Rusty and Adam had already bonded and he was the odd man out. "Do what he says." He tucked his dick into his underwear, settled his jeans back onto his hips then sat on the blanket.

"What's wrong?" Rusty asked.

Manny picked up his sandwich. "I'm hungry," he answered. He wasn't going to tell Rusty how much the simple exchange with Adam had hurt him or how his biggest fears about the situation were coming to fruition. He took a bite and did his best to chew the roast beef before swallowing.

"Manny?" Adam sounded alarmed.

Anger filled Manny at the tone of Adam's voice. He hadn't been the one to initiate the sexually charged situation, but it seemed Adam assumed he was the one at fault. He tilted his head back and stared up at the stars overhead. It could have been the perfect first date. "Don't worry. I won't touch him," he told Adam.

"Just wait until I get there," Adam replied. "Is Rusty waiting for me at the door?"

Rusty got to his feet, and Manny couldn't help but notice how cute he looked in his white tube socks and plaid boxers. He shook his head. "Go on," he urged.

Rusty shot out of the planetarium as if he was running from a lunatic.

"He's on his way." Manny dropped the sandwich in the basket before packing up the rest of the food. He found his discarded shirt and pulled it on, wondering how the night had gone so wrong. One thing had become certain. Despite Adam's protests otherwise, Adam wanted Rusty for himself.

* * * *

Rusty pushed open the heavy door. "I'm glad you're here. I've made him mad, and I'm not sure what I did." After he'd hit it off so well with Adam, Rusty had hoped the same would happen with Manny, and it had for a while. He'd known his inexperience would be a problem, but after the way Adam had so gently taught him how to kiss, he'd thought they would be the perfect teachers to show him more.

"Calm down." Adam wrapped his arms around Rusty. "What happened?"

"I don't know." Rusty quickly played through the evening's events. "We had a good time gathering the samples. Then we came here, and started to have dinner. I asked him why he hadn't tried to kiss me, and things kind of took off from there. I can't explain it, but the way my body reacted to his scared me. Not in a bad way, but it was so intense, and I didn't know what to do, and when I asked him, and you were talking to me, too, he just shut down. Now he's mad, and I don't know why." He knew he was rambling and most of what he'd just explained probably didn't make sense to Adam any more than it made sense to him.

Adam gave Rusty a quick kiss. "Okay. First of all, Manny probably didn't kiss you because kissing makes him horny, extremely horny," he added. "He knows you're a virgin, and I warned him repeatedly to take things slow, but that's not easy for him to do."

"I wanted to touch him," Rusty confessed. "He's so beautiful."

Adam grinned. "Yeah, he is." He steered Rusty toward the theater.

They were almost at the door when Manny stepped out, carrying the picnic basket.

"Where're you going?" Adam asked.

"To the lab. I need to process those samples." Manny gestured over his shoulder. "The two of you should stay and enjoy the show."

Rusty knew if Manny left, the three of them would have no future together, which meant, he'd be left behind. He didn't want that. "Please don't go. I'm sorry I made you angry." He pulled away from Adam and took a step toward Manny. "I wanted to touch you so much, but I didn't know how, and I was afraid you wouldn't like what I did, and you'd change your mind about me."

Manny released his hold on the basket and reached for Rusty. "My anger has nothing to do with you not touching me," he growled as he squeezed Rusty against his chest. "It's our first date, and I already feel like an outsider." His gaze went to Adam. "Knowing that you feel you have to protect Rusty from me hurt."

Adam made a noise Rusty couldn't decipher before moving to press himself against Manny's back. "I'm sorry. It surprised me, and yeah, I guess it made me a little jealous when you called and asked me to bring over the lube. I didn't think Rusty was prepared for that, and it made me nervous that you'd push things too far and scare him away."

The last thing Rusty wanted was to cause trouble between Adam and Manny. "You're not going to scare me away. I'm one of those people who take forever to make a decision, but once I do, I try not to hold back. I realized after Adam and I spent time together today that I like being kissed and touched, and I wanted more. Heck, I want everything."

Adam kissed Manny's neck. "Let's go back inside," he whispered. "Let me show Rusty how you liked to be touched."

Rusty's cock hardened in response to Manny's deep growl. He reached up and cupped Manny's cheek. "Please give me another chance."

Without warning, Manny grabbed a handful of Rusty's hair and pulled his head back. "I've been waiting all evening to do this," he said before slamming his mouth down on Rusty's.

Rusty opened as Manny's tongue ravaged his mouth in the hottest kiss he'd experienced yet. Although Adam was an excellent kisser, Manny was a god. Rusty moaned when he felt something hard press against his stomach.

Manny released his hold on Rusty's hair and lifted him off the ground. "Wrap your legs around me," he grunted before taking Rusty's mouth in another series of pillaging kisses.

Rusty did as instructed and gasped when Manny's big hands cupped his ass through the thin cotton of his boxers.

"So hot," Adam said as he moved around to hold Rusty from behind. "I knew the two of you would be sexy to watch."

A wet warmth landed on Rusty's back and he knew Adam was licking him. "Naked," he said, tearing his mouth from Manny's.

There was a flurry of movement and within seconds, Rusty was lowered to the blanket. Without a moment's hesitation, Rusty pushed his underwear down and stepped out of them, exposing himself to the two hottest men he knew.

"Fuck!" Adam yelled when he got twisted in his clothes in an attempt to rid himself of the offending garments.

Laughing, Rusty did his best to help by tugging off Adam's worn athletic shoes. By the time Adam and Manny were naked, all three of them collapsed onto the blanket. Rusty wasn't sure where to look first, but he knew exactly what he wanted to feel. Gone was the shy virgin he'd been only a day earlier as he wrapped his hand around Manny's cock before searching the pile of tangled limbs for Adam's shaft.

"Kiss me," Adam ordered as he thrust against Rusty's hand.

Rusty opened for the sweep of Adam's tongue. *Perfect.* When he felt a warm mouth envelop his erection, he forgot all about the kiss and turned his attention to the top of Manny's head. "Oh, my God," he gasped.

"Feels good, doesn't it?" Adam asked, running his fingertips down Rusty's chest.

"I think I'm going to come," Rusty announced.

Manny released Rusty's cock and stared up the length of Rusty's body to meet his gaze. "*Déjame probarte.*"

"You want to taste me?" Rusty swallowed. He'd pictured himself learning how to give blow jobs, but he'd never expected men as masculine as Adam and

Manny to give him one in return. "Do you guys do that?"

Adam chuckled. "Are you joking? It's one of our favorite things to do to each other." He smoothed Manny's thick black hair away from his face. "Manny likes giving almost as much as receiving."

Manny nodded his head in agreement before taking the crown of Rusty's dick into his mouth once again.

"I've never…" Rusty started.

"We know. That's why after you fill Manny's mouth with the sweet taste of your cum, I'm going to show you how to do it back to him."

The thought of stretching his lips around Manny's huge shaft sent Rusty over the edge before he had time to shout a warning. "Sorry," he apologized as the first volley of cum shot from his cock.

"Shhh," Adam soothed, moving down to kneel beside Manny. He bumped his shoulder against Manny's. "Let me in for a taste."

Rusty jerked as another shot of seed erupted just as Manny moved and Adam captured Rusty's crown with his mouth. "Yes!" Rusty cried.

Manny scooted up and kissed Rusty, although instead of taking control, he opened his mouth for Rusty to explore.

Rusty took advantage and thoroughly enjoyed the taste of himself on Manny's tongue. It felt so wicked, yet the simple act of sharing the after-effect of his orgasm was intoxicating. He barely cut off a whimper when Manny broke the kiss.

"*Vale la pena esperar,*" Manny rumbled.

Worth the wait. Rusty felt the heat of his blush. "Thank you."

"Manny's turn," Adam announced.

"I have a better idea. Why don't I show Rusty how you like it then I...we can show him how we fuck," Manny suggested.

Rusty refused to point out that he'd already seen the pair fuck, so he nodded in agreement. As sated as he was after being sucked off, he didn't care what they did as long as it involved being naked and together.

Chapter Four

Running behind schedule, Rusty threw open the front door of BK House and almost ran over Charlie, the house manager. "Sorry."

"Where've you been? I was worried sick about you when you didn't come home last night," Charlie huffed.

Although Charlie tried not to pry into their personal business, he'd started hovering since Rusty's attack.

"I was on a date," Rusty announced. "A really good one."

"It's almost eight in the morning, I'd say it must have been a good one." Charlie tried to hide his smile. "Are you going to tell me who you were with?"

Rusty knew of several students who dated members of the faculty, but he didn't know of anyone dating two professors at the same time. "Someone from class," he replied with a half-truth. "Sorry, but if I don't jump in the shower, I'm going to be late for lab." He started up the stairs, but he didn't get far before Charlie called after him.

"There was another attack last night outside Clean Slate. Make sure you don't go back there alone," Charlie warned.

The news knocked the air out of Rusty and he sank to sit on a step, struggling to draw a simple breath into his lungs. "Was it anyone I know?"

"No, some guy from town, from what I understand. Chase said the owners are going to hire a few security guards to patrol the parking lot until they catch the assholes."

Charlie's worry over Rusty's all-night date made more sense. "I'm sorry I worried you," Rusty apologized.

"Just do me a favor and call next time. At least until these attacks stop."

"I will." Rusty grabbed the banister and pulled himself to his feet. After the night he'd spent with Manny and Adam, he'd thought he'd be floating for days, but knowing someone else had been attacked set him on edge once again. "Talk to you later, Charlie. Let me know if you hear anything more."

For the first time since Chase had started dating Mac, Rusty was grateful to have the room to himself. He fell back on his bed and stared at the ceiling. He couldn't have asked for a better introduction to the world of dating, and even though Adam and Manny had decided the three of them needed a few more days before they fucked him, Rusty had argued otherwise. Watching Manny fuck Adam close up was a lot different from the time he'd caught the two of them in their bedroom. Not only had they included him, but Manny had shown Rusty the proper way to prepare Adam's hole before fucking.

Rusty glanced down at his erection. He'd come three times within a twelve-hour period, and his body was still aching for more. He had a break between his lab and Adam's class. Perhaps they wouldn't mind if he stopped by their office. He grinned as he undressed and wrapped a towel around his waist.

He stepped into the hall and was forced to wait while two freshman unlocked the door to their room.

"Yeah, man, I heard he was fucked up by the time some security dude saw what was happening and ran to help. Fucker got away *again*." Robby, one of the younger men, stopped talking when he noticed Rusty. "Sorry."

"There was another attack?" Rusty asked, glancing over his shoulder to make sure no one was coming up behind him.

"Yeah. The guy got it a lot worse than you did though," Robby continued. "From what I heard, the fucker used a bottle instead of his fist. The man who was attacked is still in the hospital with a fractured cheekbone and a long gash down the side of his face."

Rusty began to walk backward toward his room. Forget the shower. No way could he stand behind that curtain, knowing anyone could sneak up on him.

* * * *

Rusty was on his way across the quad toward the science building when he noticed someone following him. He tucked his chin down and walked faster.

"Icarus Bonham?" the stranger called after him.

No. No. No. Rusty's pulse began to race as he took off at a run. Few people knew his real name, and there was only one reason a stranger would know it. He'd tried to ignore the threatening emails sent by his mother's family, praying they would get tired of harassing him and move on. The night of the attack, he'd worried that his aunt had sent the thugs after him, but he'd eventually convinced himself he was simply in the wrong place at the wrong time.

"Stop!" the man yelled.

Rusty glanced over his shoulder as he ran up the steps of the science building. The stranger was gaining on him. *Dammit!* He pushed open the door and didn't stop running until he reached Manny and Adam's office. "Let me in!" He pounded his fist on the door while watching the hallways for any sign of his attacker.

The door swung open and a scowling Manny filled the frame. "What's wrong?" he asked, his arms going around Rusty's waist.

Rusty pointed to the stairs as he tried to catch his breath. "Someone's chasing me."

Manny gently pushed Rusty inside the office. "Lock the door."

"You can't go after him by yourself," Rusty argued.

"What is he wearing?" Manny asked.

Rusty tried to think. "Umm, he had on a long black trench coat and a blue and red baseball cap."

"I'll take care of it, *bebé*. You stay here. Adam should be by in a few minutes."

Before Rusty could protest further, Manny left the office, pulling the door closed behind him. Rusty called Adam.

"Hey," Adam answered.

"Are you in the science building?" Rusty hated the thought of Manny getting hurt because of him.

"Yeah. I'm on my way up to the office."

"There was a guy chasing me across the quad, and now Manny's gone after him," Rusty said in a rush.

"Good," Adam replied.

"Good? What if he gets hurt?" Rusty couldn't believe Adam wasn't as worried about Manny as he was.

"Manny's a fourth degree black belt in Jujutsu. Feel sorry for the punk he's hunting not him."

"I'm sorry, but that doesn't make me feel any better. What if the assailant has a gun or a knife?"

"I'm at the door, and you've been watching too many cop shows."

Rusty heard Adam's key in the lock and was right there when Adam stepped into the office. He wrapped his arms around Adam and buried his face against Adam's collarbone. "I was on the way to the lab, but when he called my name and took off after me, I ran straight here."

Adam ran his hands soothingly up and down Rusty's back. "I'm glad you did."

"Did you hear there was another attack last night at Clean Slate?"

"Yeah. My TA mentioned it. Do you think it was the same guy who chased you?"

"That's what doesn't make sense to me," Rusty began. "The man in the quad called me by my real name. As far as I know, there are only about four or five people here who know my name. I realize this may sound crazy, but I've been getting some really nasty emails from my mom's sister and her family. What if the attack at the club and the man in the quad are working for them?"

Adam buried his fingers in Rusty's hair. "There's a whole lot of information I'm going to need to be filled in on, but we should wait for Manny." He led Rusty to the sofa. "You want some water?"

"Sure." Rusty hadn't realized until he went to sit down that he still had his messenger bag slung over his shoulder. He dropped his books to the floor and sat on the edge of the couch without taking his eyes off the door. "I should've gone to campus security instead of involving Manny."

"Bullshit." Adam handed Rusty a bottle of water. "Manny would've never forgiven you if you hadn't come to us." He sat next to Rusty. "Manny's not always vocal about the way he feels, but you'll always know he cares by his actions."

When the door opened, Rusty jumped to his feet. He quickly scanned Manny for injuries. "You didn't catch him, did you?"

Manny shut the door. "I caught him." He rubbed the back of his neck. "He's not your attacker. He's a process server."

"Why would he be looking for me?" Rusty sank to the sofa as realization dawned on him. "My aunt's suing me for part of my parent's estate," he surmised.

"He would not tell me, but he asked if I knew where Icarus Bonham lived. Evidently, whoever hired him doesn't have your current address." Manny exchanged glances with Adam. "And we do not have your real name."

"I would've told you eventually. I stopped using the name when I left home, but my mom and dad still called me Ic until they died. As you can imagine, growing up, I was known as Icky, and when I moved here, I didn't want my past to follow me." Rusty took a sip of his water. "But it seems no matter where I go, my past finds me."

"Why would a process server being looking for you?" Manny asked, joining Adam and Rusty on the couch.

"I don't know for sure, but I think my aunt is trying to get some of my parents' money." Rusty knew the woman didn't have a case, and he was suddenly grateful he'd kept the worst of the emails. "My Aunt Virginia is my mom's older sister. When I went home after the accident, I found her sitting at the kitchen table my dad had made for my mom's thirtieth birthday." Rusty shook his head. "I don't know how she got in, she wouldn't tell me, but I told myself that it wasn't the time to start an argument. It wasn't until she started demanding that she take possession of my mom's body for a proper burial that I'd had enough. I made arrangements with the funeral home to have both my parents cremated." He glanced at Manny. "That's what they wanted," he explained. "While the funeral home took care of the details, I made arrangements to sell the house and pack up everything that was important to me for storage."

"So you think your aunt is suing you because you had them cremated?" Adam asked.

"No." Rusty leaned his head against Adam's shoulder. "It's about the money. I have it, and she wants it." He shrugged. "At least part of it."

"Is she legally entitled to any of it?" Manny asked.

"No. My mother hated her family." Rusty knew he needed to explain further. He didn't want Manny and Adam to think his mom was just being stingy. "Technically, my dad was homeless when he married my mom. He wasn't living on the streets or anything, but he'd sold everything he owned to buy a small piece of land in the town where I grew up. It was only twenty acres, but he knew there was oil underneath it."

"And he wanted the oil?" Adam asked.

For some reason, the question made Rusty chuckle. "No. The opposite. He didn't want anyone drilling on that land because he said it was too pretty to ruin.

Anyway, he sold the house his parents had left him, sold his car, cashed out his college fund and bought it. He'd lived in a tent on the land for almost two years before he asked my mom to marry him. She said yes, but her family said no. They told her if she married him, she would be dead to them." He sighed, remembering the way his mother had looked at his father every time he'd come into a room. "She loved him more than anything."

"Then, when your dad started making money, her family changed their minds," Manny surmised.

"Yeah." Rusty looked from Manny to Adam. "Until that day in the kitchen, I'd never even met my aunt because my mom refused to give them another chance. There's no way she promised them part of the estate like my Aunt Virginia claims. No way."

"Did they have a will?" Adam ran his hand up and down Rusty's back.

"Sure. That's why I don't understand why a process server would be looking for me, but I know that has to be it. When my family died, I sent out an email, informing their friends of the tragedy. Aunt Virginia must have gotten my email address from one of them because I've been receiving pleading messages from my aunt and about five cousins I've never met. I've tried to ignore them, but they've gotten pretty nasty over the last few months."

Manny rubbed his hand over his jaw. "I think we need to find that process server and fight this thing head on. Going to court may be the only way to get rid of them once and for all."

Rusty nodded. "I didn't run from him because I didn't want to be served. I thought—"

"Yeah, honey, we know," Adam said, cutting Rusty off.

* * * *

"With all the names out there for your parents to choose from, why Icarus?" Adam poured the lasagna noodles into a colander.

Seated on the kitchen island, Rusty put the court documents aside. He still couldn't believe Virginia was suing him for nearly three million dollars and the first piece of land his father had purchased. Although Adam's question had come out of nowhere, it was perfectly timed. "It was a warning of sorts. My parents spent the early years of their marriage protesting and taking on big corporations. They believed money and greed made a man's soul wither and die. Do you know the story of Icarus?"

Adam glanced up from the lasagna he was assembling. "Yeah. Icarus had feathers made of wax and when he flew too close to the sun, the wax melted and he plunged to earth and died."

"My dad said that Icarus should have been content with the ability to fly because it was more than most people could do, but he was greedy and wanted more. Icarus believed he was invincible so he challenged the sun and lost."

"So he was warning you not to take on the big corporations?" Adam shook his head. "That doesn't make sense given what you've told me about them."

"No, I think for my dad, the sun was money. He was trying to tell me to be happy with what I had because if all I thought about was money, I'd lose everything in the end." Rusty sighed. "I can't explain it. I mean, he had money, a lot of it, but he was happy living the simple life. He didn't work hours in the garage to make money, he did it to save the environment. The money was a way of making sure the corporations didn't destroy the beauty of the world around us."

"What do you think he would say about the lawsuit?" Adam asked.

"I think the whole thing would've made him sick to his stomach, but I've been trying to figure out what he'd do in my shoes. I know he would have fought her over the land, but the money has me stumped."

"Doesn't really matter though, does it? I mean, Virginia doesn't have a case," Adam pointed out.

"No, she doesn't," Rusty agreed. "There's a part of me that wants to go after her and her kids for harassing me. That's what I'm worried about. I don't know what they're capable of. What if my dad was wrong and the sun isn't money at all but vengeance. I'm not sure winning the lawsuit will be enough for me by the time it's over. Will the whole process change me?" He nodded. "I have a feeling it will. Knowing that, do I fight it and go after Virginia and her family or save myself and settle?" Rusty took off his glasses and cleaned them with the bottom of his T-shirt. "Is preserving who I am worth a few million dollars?"

Before Adam could answer, Manny stepped into the room. He looked from Adam to Rusty and without a word, he scooped Rusty off the island and into his arms. "Put dinner in the oven and join us in the living room," he told Adam as he carried Rusty to the deep sofa.

Settled comfortably on Manny's lap, Rusty closed his eyes. He knew Manny wanted to talk, but that's the last thing he wanted to do. "Just hold me."

"*Sí*," Manny replied, kissing Rusty's temple.

It had only been a few days, and Rusty had already grown addicted to the possessive way Manny held him. He tilted his chin back and kissed the light brown skin of Manny's throat. "Thank you."

Manny rubbed Rusty's hip with his palm and the simple gesture sent sexual sparks through Rusty's body. It seemed Manny's protective instinct wasn't the only thing he was becoming addicted to. "How long does it take to bake lasagna?"

"Forty to forty-five minutes." Manny squeezed Rusty's ass. "Do you need some attention?"

Rusty still wasn't used to asking for what he wanted from Manny and Adam, even though they'd tried their best to hammer it into his head. "Yes." He sat up and pulled off his shirt, barely saving his glasses in the process.

Manny stood with Rusty still in his arms and lowered Rusty's feet to the floor. He held Rusty's gaze as he untied the drawstring of his scrub pants and let them fall.

"You're not wearing underwear," Rusty pointed out as he pushed his jeans and boxers down. He kicked the denim to the side before pulling off his socks.

"I never do in the lab," Manny answered as he rid himself of the rest of his clothes. He set off toward the bedroom, and Rusty wondered if he was supposed to follow.

"Tell Adam to turn off the oven. This might take a while," Manny said before disappearing into the hallway.

Naked, Rusty walked into the kitchen. "Manny said to turn off the oven." He smiled. "I think he's hungry for something else right now."

Adam's gaze fixed on Rusty's erection. "I think you're both hungry for something else." Already bare-chested, he began to unbutton his jeans as he stalked toward Rusty. "Anything in particular you'd like to try this evening?"

Rusty had thought about being with the two men on and off all day. He reached behind him and drew his hands down his lower back to land on the cheeks of his ass. "I want to be touched here," he confessed. "I want to know if I'll ever be ready to do what you and Manny did last night."

Adam continued to move until his lightly furred chest pressed against Rusty. "You want us to play with your ass?"

"Do you mind?" Rusty asked.

Adam squeezed Rusty's ass. "Baby, I've wanted your ass since the first day I saw you."

"Get in here," Manny called from the living room.

Adam gave Rusty a deep kiss before releasing him. "Go to Manny and let him get started. I have to put a few things away and turn off the oven."

Before leaving the kitchen, Rusty cupped Adam's erection. "You'll join us soon, right?"

"Absolutely." Adam gave Rusty's butt a playful slap. "Go."

Rusty turned and made his way back to the living room. Manny was sitting on the couch with a towel under him and another dampened towel on the floor beside his feet. "Come here, *bebé*."

Nervous about what was to come, Rusty straddled Manny's lap.

"He wants us to play with his ass!" Adam shouted from the kitchen.

Mortified, Rusty tried to hide his embarrassment by burying his face against Manny's shoulder.

"No." Manny grabbed a handful of Rusty's hair and tilted his head back until Rusty was forced to meet

Manny's gaze. "There is no shame in asking for what you need."

Rusty wondered if all men were as forthcoming about their desires as Manny and Adam expected him to be. "I'm not used to talking about this stuff."

"That will need to change because Adam and I enjoy sex, and neither of us are afraid to ask the other for what we want." Manny retrieved a bottle of lube from the end table and held it up.

Astroglide Sensual Strawberry. "Flavored lube?" Rusty wasn't aware they even made it.

"I could eat strawberries all day and night." Manny sucked Rusty's bottom lip into his mouth before releasing it. He tipped the bottle onto its side and poured a bit of the slick onto his fingers.

"Does it taste as good as it smells?" Rusty asked.

"Not quite, but it's better than most." Manny set the bottle back onto the table before spreading his legs farther apart.

The action not only spread Rusty's cheeks apart but also exposed his pucker to the cool air. Whether it was the cold or his excitement, he wasn't sure, but he shivered, his skin breaking out into gooseflesh. He held his breath as Manny's finger brushed across his virgin hole several times before pressing against the pucker until the tip pushed inside. Rusty gasped at the sensation. It felt better than anything he'd ever experienced, including kissing and coming.

"Oh, my God," Rusty moaned.

"You like that?" Adam asked, dropping down on the sofa beside Manny.

Rusty started to answer just as Manny pushed deeper inside him. His mouth fell open as his body trembled at the invasion. There were no words to describe how he felt at that moment, so he simply nodded.

"*Usted es tan fuerte, bebé,*" Manny growled in Rusty's ear.

You are so tight, baby. Rusty played the sentence repeatedly in his head as Manny slowly slid his finger in and out. He glanced down and watched as his leaking cock painted a trail of pre-cum across Manny's dark-skinned torso. "This is my new favorite thing," he announced, sharing the conclusion he'd come to earlier.

Manny grunted, and Adam laughed before leaning over to give Rusty a deep kiss. "I think you've made Manny very happy. I like to be fucked, but foreplay isn't my favorite thing unless it's done quickly." He grinned. "Manny," he began, moving to kiss Manny softly before continuing, "would love to sit and watch an entire soccer game while indulging in foreplay."

"I hate soccer, but I'd be willing to sit through it if I had Manny's finger handy." Rusty felt his face heat with embarrassment. "I can't believe I said that out loud."

Adam ran his hand down Rusty's butt. "In that case, you can keep Manny company on Saturdays. He'd rather watch soccer on his days off, and I prefer to get out of the house and enjoy the world."

Rusty knew how much Adam had enjoyed the hike they'd taken together earlier in the week, and he didn't want Adam to think otherwise. "I can still go hiking with you once in a while, right?"

"I'd like that." Adam grabbed the bottle of lube and dripped a thin line down the crack of Rusty's ass.

Manny used the fresh supply of slick to introduce a second finger into Rusty's hole.

Rusty sucked in a breath at the slight burn. He understood it was part of the process, but he hadn't been expecting Manny to work up to more than one digit so quickly.

"Just relax." Adam kissed Rusty's neck. "The more you give in to the invasion, the easier it is to take."

Rusty turned his head and captured Adam's lips in a kiss. He swept his tongue into Adam's mouth and moaned at the spicy taste of pasta sauce. Unlike many people, Adam made his sauce from scratch. He'd told Rusty he'd learned from his grandmother how to make gravy, as he called it, the right way. He pulled back. "Mmm. You taste good."

"Is that your way of telling me you're hungry?"

"Of course he is hungry. He didn't eat lunch," Manny replied.

"Do I have to get off Manny's lap to eat?" Rusty asked. He rested his head on Manny's shoulder. He was more relaxed than he'd been since leaving the apartment that morning.

"I'll go turn the oven back on." Adam stood and headed toward the kitchen, leaving Manny and Rusty alone once again.

Rusty began to kiss Manny's jaw. "Am I ready yet?"

"*Sí*, but it will be uncomfortable the first time," Manny warned. "Are you sure you want this?"

If Manny's fingers had the power to turn him into a pile of blissful goo, Rusty couldn't imagine how good his cock would feel. "So ready."

Manny removed his fingers and wiped them on the damp towel at his feet, holding Rusty in place with one strong arm. "Hand me that lube."

Rusty picked up the bottle and waited for further instructions. "You never tasted it," he reminded Manny.

"Some other time." Manny reached between them and held his shaft by the base. "Drip some over me."

Rusty tilted the bottle and watched as drops of the clear shiny liquid dropped onto the crown of Manny's erection before sliding down his length. "Like that?"

"Perfect." Manny ran his palm up and down his shaft several times as Rusty continued to pour. "That's good."

Rusty replaced the cap and set the bottle on the table. "Adam?" he called, wanting Adam to be there for his first time.

"Coming." Adam rushed into the room, but instead of sitting on the couch, he sat on the coffee table behind Rusty. "Let me feel you," he said a moment before he touched the stretched skin of Rusty's hole. "Fuck," he groaned. "Go easy on him, Manny, because I'm going to want in later."

Manny grunted in reply. "Lean forward on your knees. I will let you have control this time."

This time? Rusty grinned. It turned him on when Manny went all alpha male. He did as instructed and waited. When he felt the head of Manny's erection press against him, he pushed back against it. Frustration filled him when nothing happened. "I'm not doing it right"

"Push out," Adam moved to whisper in Rusty's ear. "And relax."

Rusty wondered how the heck he was supposed to relax and concentrate on what he was doing at the same time. He leaned back again and wiggled his ass a bit as he applied more pressure and was rewarded when he felt Manny's crown push inside. He gasped as his body fought to accommodate the intrusion.

"Easy," Manny crooned, holding Rusty in place. "Don't move until the pain subsides."

While part of Rusty wanted to slam back and get the discomfort over with, the more intelligent part of his brain told him to follow Manny's suggestion. He wrapped his arms around Manny's neck. "Then you'd better kiss me to distract me."

Manny tilted his head and covered Rusty's lips with his own. Like with most of their encounters, Manny pushed his tongue into Rusty's mouth as he took charge of the situation. The longer they kissed, the hornier Rusty became and before he could stop himself, he moved, taking more of Manny's length inside him.

"Oh, shit, the two of you are sexy together," Adam groaned.

Manny broke the kiss and leaned his forehead against Rusty's. "Suck Adam's cock while I fuck you."

Rusty turned and crooked his finger at Adam as Manny eased more of his shaft into Rusty's ass.

Adam stepped up onto the sofa and guided his cock toward Rusty's open mouth. Rusty could only imagine what the three of them must look like at the moment. After catching Manny and Adam together the weekend of his attack, Rusty had watched several videos featuring threesomes, but he'd always felt bad for the guy who looked like he was being used by the other two. Now that he had Manny's cock in his butt and Adam's in his mouth, he realized he was the lucky one of the three of them, not the other way around. He decided right then that what he'd told Chase was wrong. Being the meat in the middle of a professor sandwich was actually the perfect place for him to be.

Rusty released Adam's dick and cried out when Manny thrust the rest of the way inside. "Damn!" he ground out. He closed his eyes and took deep breaths, letting them out slowly each time. After several moments, the pain eased. He swiveled his hips, testing the foreign object that impaled him. While it felt okay, for some reason, it wasn't at all as pleasurable as being fingered was.

Manny grabbed the cheeks of Rusty's ass and pulled out only to thrust in again. Rusty waited, praying the pleasure would slam into him like in the videos he'd watched, but it didn't. He felt his eyes fill with tears as he fought to stay in control of himself as Manny continued to move in and out of him. He hated the direction his thoughts had taken, but if he were honest, he was underwhelmed. Shame filled him as he returned his attention to Adam's cock. Hopefully, he could ride out the experience without giving his true feelings away because if Manny and Adam found out he didn't care for anal intercourse, they probably wouldn't have much use for him anymore, and the last thing he wanted was to lose them. He licked the head of Adam's shaft before easing the length between his lips. The truth hit him just as the first tear escaped.

"Manny! Stop!" Adam yelled, pulling his erection out of Rusty's mouth. He knelt on the sofa beside Rusty. "What's wrong, baby?"

Rusty couldn't even look at Adam as tears began to roll down his face. How did he admit that something as exquisite as Manny's cock didn't feel as good as it looked? Simple, he couldn't do it. No way would he hurt a man who had been so loving toward him.

"Talk to me, baby," Adam urged, wiping Rusty's tears with the pads of his thumbs.

Rusty lifted his chin and met Adam's gaze. There was so much tenderness in Adam's expression that he couldn't speak. He'd been so afraid Manny and Adam would hurt him, and that he hadn't even considered the possibility that he'd be the one to damage any chance of a relationship. Without a word to either men, he dislodged Manny's dick, grabbed his clothes and fled to the safety of the bathroom.

Chapter Five

Manny didn't say a word as he got to his feet. He did a quick clean-up with the towel before pulling on his scrubs and his T-shirt. "I'm sorry," he said to Adam before grabbing his shoes.

"Where're you going?" Adam asked as Manny stalked toward the door.

"He was not ready, and I pushed him." Manny shoved his bare feet into his sneakers. "My fault," he admonished himself before pulling on his coat and leaving the apartment.

Adam climbed off the couch and wandered into the kitchen. He stared at the oven and wondered if he should turn it off for a second time. *No*, he decided. They would need to eat after he figured out what the fuck had happened. He mentally went through the last few minutes in his mind in an effort to make sense of it. When Manny had eased his way inside Rusty, Adam had made sure to watch Rusty closely for signs of pain. Other than a few winces, there appeared to be only once that Rusty actually hurt, but that had seemed to subside quickly. What bothered Adam the most was the blank expression on Rusty's face up until the moment Adam had noticed the tears. "It doesn't make sense," he said to the empty room.

He found his jeans in the living room and pulled them on. Without bothering to button them, he walked down the hall and knocked on the bathroom door. "Rusty?"

"I'm sorry," Rusty replied. "God, I'm so sorry I did that."

When it became obvious that Rusty wasn't going to open the door, Adam slid down the wall to sit on the floor. "Talk to me, baby, tell me what happened." He hated to accuse Manny of causing Rusty pain, but he had to ask. "Did Manny hurt you?"

"No," Rusty said so softly Adam barely heard it.

"Did it scare you?" Adam tried to keep his voice calm, but he felt anything but.

"Not for the reason you think."

"Tell me why you were scared?" Adam prompted.

"I didn't like it, and I know how important it is to you and Manny, and I was there, and I didn't like it, and I didn't know what I was supposed to do about it because I don't want to lose the two of you."

Adam got to his feet. Rusty's ramblings were so full of heartache that Adam felt his own eyes sting with unshed tears. "Let me in. Please, baby, just let me in," he begged.

The door opened and Rusty stepped out into the hall.

Adam immediately enveloped Rusty in a tight embrace. He tried to keep the hurt out of his voice when he asked, "Do you really believe Manny and I want you only so we can fuck you?"

Rusty shook his head but didn't meet Adam's gaze. "No, but I know sex is part of it. You've both told me that you want me."

"Yeah, because we do, but sticking my cock in your ass isn't the only thing I'm after." Adam knew he sounded pissed, but in a way, he was. "We want you. Not just a willing hole. I've already told you, many have offered, and we've turned every single one of them down because you're the only other person we want in our bed and in our lives."

"It didn't hurt me, so I can still do it once in a while if you need me to," Rusty mumbled.

"Anal sex is only one way to show someone you love how much you care for them." Adam loved to fuck, so he knew it might become harder to connect to Rusty on an intimate level, but he also enjoyed giving and receiving blow jobs, and the two of them had already proven to each other how much they liked to kiss. It might not always be enough, but it was enough for the moment, at least until they could deepen their emotional relationship. "Manny left," he informed Rusty. "I think he feels he did something that'll drive you away."

"I don't want to go away," Rusty replied. "I just wanted so much to like it, but when I didn't, I didn't know what to do."

"There's nothing wrong with that. I don't like Manny's tongue in my ass. It took me almost a year before I finally admitted it to him." Adam wiped a dangling tear from Rusty's long red eyelashes. "Guess what? Our relationship didn't fall apart over it. We simply agreed that if I ever did want him to do it to me again, I would ask, and until then, we'd find other things to do with each other."

Hope sparkled in Rusty's puffy eyes. "Do you really think we can work something out?"

Adam's chest ached at the question. The heart that had belonged to Manny since their third date opened just enough to allow Rusty to slip inside in that moment. "Yes, baby, I'm sure we can work it out."

"What about Manny? Do you think he'll feel the same way?"

Adam was damn near sure of it, but he couldn't answer for Manny. "When he's down on himself, he goes to the lake because, according to him, cleaning up that shithole is the only good thing he's ever done in his life." He gave Rusty a soft peck on the lips. "Take my Jeep and go talk to him."

"Without you?"

"You and I have had our talk and worked it out. Now it's time for you and Manny to work it out. Once you do, come home and eat the fucking lasagna that I've spent hours preparing."

Rusty grinned. "Have I ever told you how much I love lasagna? My mom didn't make it, but there's this little restaurant back home that does, and it was always my favorite place to go on special occasions."

Adam cupped Rusty face in his hands and leaned down for a tender, yet deep, kiss. "Go. Bring our man home."

* * * *

Manny filled two more gallon jugs with lake water and carried them back to his car, stowing them beside the others. He wasn't surprised when he spotted Adam's Jeep slow and turn into the property.

The Jeep came to a stop a few feet from Manny, and Rusty stepped out. "Hey," Rusty greeted.

Manny stiffened, wondering if Rusty had come in person to break it off. "Where's Adam?"

"At home waiting dinner for us." Rusty rounded the front of the Jeep and moved to stand next to the open trunk. "I'm sorry I ran out like that. Even more sorry that you felt you'd done something wrong."

"I obviously did," Manny replied, shutting the trunk.

"No, you didn't, there's something I need to tell you, and I really need you to just let me get it out before you say anything."

Manny leaned back against the sedan with his arms crossed over his chest. "Okay." He prepared himself for the worst as Rusty began to talk, but it didn't take long for understanding to dawn on him. Although he'd heard of men who didn't care for anal sex, he'd never come across one. Most men that he'd taken to bed had been more than eager to feel the full length and circumference of his cock. Discovering that Rusty received more pleasure from a simple touch as opposed to a big dick didn't hurt Manny's feelings in the least. However, he could tell by the way Rusty's voice was getting higher in pitch that Rusty was worried about Manny's reaction.

Manny knew Adam would have a harder time with the limited restriction to Rusty's ass, but according to Rusty, Adam had said they could find other ways to express their desire for each other.

"So, I guess what I need to know is if not fucking me is a deal breaker?" Rusty finally asked.

Manny grabbed Rusty under the arms and lifted him to sit on the trunk. Once they were finally eye to eye, he caged Rusty in with hands on either side of his slim hips and leaned in until their noses almost touched.

"That depends. I don't like vegetables. Is that a deal breaker for you?"

Rusty shook his head. "Although, you really need vegetables to stay healthy. Are you at least taking vitamin supplements?"

* * * *

Rusty picked at his thumbnail as he read the latest email from his cousin Carl. In it, Carl listed all of Aunt Virginia's health problems that, according to Aunt Virginia, were a direct result of the stress caused by Rusty's refusal to give his mother's family the money they were promised.

Tired of it all, he closed his laptop. It was the first time in two weeks that he'd come directly to BK House after class, and the only reason he'd done so that day was because he needed to think about the lawsuit. As much as he loved spending all his free time with Adam and Manny, his brain tended to shut down the moment either of them touched him.

"Come in," he responded to the knock on the door.

Locky stuck his head in the room. "Jack wants to know if you're staying for dinner?"

Jack was Charlie's partner and a darn good cook. "Yeah," Rusty replied.

Locky gestured to Chase's old bed. "You mind?"

Rusty shook his head. He didn't often get visits from Locky, so he had a pretty good guess that the dorm counselor either wanted to talk about the most recent attack or where he'd been nearly every night for the previous two weeks.

Locky shut the door and moved to sit on Chase's old bed. "How've you been?"

"Good." Great, actually, but Rusty wasn't giving anything away until he knew what Locky wanted.

"Charlie tells me you're seeing someone."

"Yes," Rusty answered.

"Anyone I know?"

Rusty stared at Locky for several moments before answering. "I can tell by your question that you already have a good idea of who I'm seeing, so why don't you just tell me how wrong I am and get it over with."

Locky reared back and held up both hands. "Whoa. Dude, where's the hostility coming from?"

Am I being hostile? Rusty bit his lower lip, realizing that he'd jumped on Locky for no reason. He glanced over his shoulder at the laptop. "Sorry. In case you haven't heard, I'm being sued, and I guess I'm on edge."

"Who the hell's suing you?" Locky asked, genuine concern in his voice.

"My aunt. She wants money. A lot of it."

"I'm sorry, Rusty, I had no idea. Do you have to go to court?"

"I don't know. I came back here after class to figure out what to do. Part of me wants to fight because she doesn't have a case, but the other part of me wants to just give her money so she'll go away and never contact me again. And, since she's suing me personally, and not the foundation my parents set up, I've even considered donating my inheritance to the foundation to stop her in her tracks."

"You're seeing Professor Ryan and Professor Corto Delgado, right?" Lucky asked.

"Yes." Rusty prepared himself for the coming lecture.

"What do they think you should do?"

Rusty hid his surprise by removing his glasses. He spent a moment cleaning them on his hem before putting them back on. "I haven't asked them what I should do, and they haven't offered an opinion."

"Do they know why you're here this evening?"

"I doubt it. I told them I had things to do, and I might see them later." Rusty wasn't sure why he was explaining himself to Locky. "Is there a problem with that?"

"No. I mean, it's your business, but if I was struggling with a decision like the one you have on your plate, I'd go to Becket."

"So you think I should talk to Becket about it?"

Locky chuckled and shook his head. "You can if you want. I just thought maybe talking to your boyfriends could help. I said that because Becket's my boyfriend."

Rusty knew Becket was more than Locky's boyfriend. The two of them were nearly inseparable lately. Still, he'd never really thought of Manny and Adam as his boyfriends. *Hi, Mr President. I'd like to introduce you to my boyfriends, Manny and Adam.* He tried it out in his head and realized he liked the sound of it. "I'm sure they'd tell me to do whatever I decide."

"That's not the point. People who care about each other share the good news and the bad. Believe me, it helps when you know someone has your back no matter what you decide," Locky explained.

Rusty considered Locky's advice. "What's Jack making for dinner?"

"It's Thursday." Locky looked at Rusty like he'd gone crazy.

"Hamburgers on the grill." Rusty couldn't believe he'd asked the question. Every Thursday, rain or shine, Jack manned the huge grill Charlie had bought him for Christmas several years ago. "Do you think he'd be mad if I skipped out?"

"Do they know about the lawsuit?"

"Charlie does, so I assume Jack does." Even though Rusty wasn't home often, he'd kept his promise and remembered to call Charlie every day.

"As long as you promise to be here for Sunday Pot Roast, I'll cover for you," Locky said with a sly grin.

"Deal." Rusty had already told Manny and Adam that he couldn't miss another Sunday dinner. "You think I could invite the professors, or would that be too weird for everyone?"

"Are you ashamed that you're dating two men?"

"No."

Locky got to his feet. "Then I don't know why anyone would feel weird. I'll let Jack know we're having an extra two for roast."

"Thanks," Rusty told Locky before he left the room. He hadn't realized how easy Locky was to talk to. He made a mental note to commend Becket on his choice of partners. He pulled out his phone and called Adam.

"Hey, baby," Adam answered.

"Have you guys eaten?"

"No, we were just arguing over pizza or Chinese. Why? You coming over early?" Adam asked.

"Actually, I'd like to take the two of you out to dinner. I need some advice on this lawsuit, so I thought we could have steak and discuss it." It was the first time Rusty had initiated a date, and he was suddenly nervous.

"As long as it's not fancy. I hate fancy. What about Outback?"

"That sounds good," Rusty agreed.

"Okay. We picking you up?"

"Yep. Is it all right if I bring a change of clothes?"

"Weekend's coming up. Pack a couple changes," Adam suggested.

Rusty brightened at the request. "I'd like that."

"Let me fill Manny in on the plan. We're still in the office, so I'm sure he's got something to clean up or turn off before we go, but we should be by in twenty minutes or so."

"I'll be ready." Rusty hung up as a sense of rightness filled him.

* * * *

"How're the fish?" Rusty asked, pulling Adam's red fuzzy blanket higher around his bare shoulders.

"Still alive," Manny replied, resettling Rusty in his lap. He'd decided to test the lake water by filling a tank in the lab and introducing goldfish. "I'll give it another week, but I feel good about ordering some bass to stock the lake."

"I'm so proud of you." Rusty nuzzled Manny's neck before flicking the pile of papers on Adam's lap with his toes. "Ready to go fishing?"

Manny thumped Rusty on the ass. "Behave." He knew the nature-loving environmentalist was teasing, but so was he. "Real Madrid plays on Saturday."

"Who?" Rusty asked, unbuttoning Manny's shirt.

"His favorite soccer team," Adam supplied, glancing up from the tests he was grading.

"What time, because I told Adam I'd check out a new trail with him?" Rusty asked, his fingers idly playing with Manny's nipple.

"Noon," Manny answered. He was still distracted by their earlier conversation. Once Rusty had opened up about the emails, Manny had been ready to get on a plane and take care of the situation once and for all. It had taken both Adam and Rusty to calm him down again enough to listen to the rest. Now that he had a clearer picture of Rusty's aunt and her children, he had suggested fighting the lawsuit to the end. Before getting the whole story, he had been in favor of settling with the woman because he'd believed Aunt Virginia must really need the money. However, he no longer felt that was the case. Virginia lived in a five-bedroom home, drove a luxury car and had a husband who made a good salary. "You need to countersue," he said.

"What?" Rusty stopped playing with Manny's nipple and looked up at him.

"Print out those emails, send them to your lawyer and countersue Virginia and her children for harassment and legal fees. I don't know what kind of mother she is, but naming her children and knowing they may lose everything because of her greed might be enough incentive for her to drop the lawsuit."

"And if it's not?" Rusty moved to straddle Manny's lap. "This could drag on for months, even years. I'm not sure I can handle that."

"You've handled your parents' unexpected deaths and being attacked." Manny brushed his lips over Rusty's. "You're a lot stronger than you give yourself credit for, and you have a good lawyer. Let him earn his money."

Rusty worried his bottom lip with his teeth. "You don't think I'll come off as stingy?"

"You don't have stingy in you, *bebé*." Manny ran his hands down Rusty's back to land on his bare ass. Since their night under the stars, Rusty had grown more and more comfortable with being naked around him and Adam. In fact, most evenings, Rusty stripped out of his clothes the moment they got home from campus.

Manny grinned when Rusty leaned against him and rested his head on Manny's shoulder. The position had become part of their nightly routine, and Manny didn't think it would be possible to be any happier with their arrangement. Although, earlier that day when Rusty announced he was going back to BK for the evening, Manny had started to feel uneasy. It wasn't that he believed Rusty was gone forever, it was merely the knowledge Rusty would be gone at all that had bothered him. He held Rusty tighter, pleased when he discovered Rusty had fallen asleep in his arms. He sighed.

"What's wrong?" Adam asked. He set down his work and scooted closer to Manny and Rusty.

Manny stared down at Adam. "Nothing, *mi cielo*." The urge to discuss their relationship with Rusty was strong, but he needed to do it when he was alone with Adam. Sweet, quirky Adam. Manny reached out and brushed the mop of wavy brown hair away from Adam's face. "Are you happy?" he whispered.

Adam's gaze moved from Manny to Rusty then back to Manny. "Very."

Manny nodded. He'd worried about Adam after they'd learned Rusty preferred foreplay. Adam had always been about the fucking, and Manny hadn't been sure Rusty and Adam would be able to create the kind of bond needed for a threesome to work without such an intimate act, but he'd been wrong. In fact, Manny got the distinct impression that Adam was enjoying the fact that Manny wasn't always after him for the foreplay he loved so much. It was more than that though. When Manny and Rusty weren't engaging in said foreplay, it was usually Adam and Rusty who were together, either kissing, hiking or discussing environmental issues. Usually, he admitted to himself, they were doing all three at the same time.

Adam ran his fingers through Rusty's thick red hair. "Are you?"

"Happy?" Manny asked. He rubbed his jaw against the top of Rusty's head. "*Sí*."

"He belongs here," Adam whispered.

"*Sí*," Manny agreed, although, he wasn't sure here was the best place for them to be. "He belongs *with* us," he corrected.

"Yeah." Adam gave Manny a deep kiss before going back to his grading. He had a teaching assistant who did most of the grading, but Adam had always insisted on reading the research papers himself. It was a grueling task that usually took up most of his time for at least two weeks after the assignments had been turned in, but Adam loved peeking into the minds of his students.

"I need you to read this one." Adam handed Manny a thin stack of papers sandwiched between two thin pieces of cardboard.

Manny examined the stack on Adam's lap and the coffee table. All of them, except the one in his hand, were bound in professional-looking plastic binders. He set the report beside him on the sofa and opened it. The moment he saw that the inside of the cover was actually cardboard from a cereal box, he knew who had written the paper. *Reuse and Recycle.* He grinned. "He should get an A just for that."

"Exactly," Adam agreed. "But I don't want to come under scrutiny by the board for favoritism. I'd like you to read it and see if you agree with the grade I gave it."

Manny gestured to the coffee table. "Hand me my glasses."

Adam retrieved the thin glasses Manny had recently been forced to buy after Rusty had caught him squinting. Adam settled the spectacles on the tip of Manny's nose. "Good?"

"*Sí.*" Manny returned his attention to Rusty's research paper, and was quickly pulled in by the subject matter.

Halfway through reading the paper on reclaiming and reconditioning environments destroyed by corporations and private citizens, Rusty stirred. "Shhh," Manny soothed, automatically moving his hand down to stroke his fingers back and forth across Rusty's hole.

Rusty settled immediately and fell back to sleep.

A sense of pride filled Manny as he read the paper. It was obvious Rusty had been moved by his efforts to clean up the plot of land he'd purchased. Rusty's per acre statistics on the labor and cost involved in reconditioning land was broken down into categories, depending upon what kind of harsh treatment the land had been subjected to. "Have you checked these figures on the number of acres still left damaged before the Reclamation Act of 1977?" he asked Adam.

"I tried, but because Rusty has avenues available to him through the foundation, I'm sure his figures are a lot closer than what I could possibly find online."

Manny shut the makeshift report cover before handing it back to Adam. Rusty's passion for the subject matter was evident in each line he wrote. "A plus." He brought the hand that had been comforting Rusty to his mouth and spit on his fingers before returning them to Rusty's hole. "In fact, I think Rusty's found his purpose in life."

"Yeah, that's what I thought."

Manny knew firsthand how much time and attention it would take Rusty to achieve his goal for a single plot of land. If Rusty did choose to follow the path he'd laid out in the research paper, he would be little more than a nomad, moving from place to place. How could they possibly make a relationship work if they were forced to spend months or even years apart?

Chapter Six

Adam entered the kitchen and headed straight to the coffee pot. Instead of spending their Sunday morning hiking, like they'd become accustomed to, he and Rusty had gone Christmas shopping for Manny's present. He poured a cup of coffee and joined Manny at the table. "Will called. He wants us to come over after dinner at the BK House."

Manny glanced up from the Sunday paper. "Rusty didn't come home with you?"

"Nope. I left him at the mall. He said he wanted to get the rest of his shopping done before the after-Thanksgiving crush." Adam took a sip of his coffee as he stole the entertainment section from Manny's pile.

"Has he told you what he plans to do after graduation?" Manny asked.

Adam glanced at Manny, or rather, the newspaper that was between him and the face he loved looking at. "He's going for his doctorate. Why?"

Manny lowered his paper. "What about after that?"

Adam finally caught on. Manny was worried about Rusty leaving them. "I don't know, but I don't think he's cut out to teach."

"Which means he'll be leaving."

Adam didn't want to consider living a life without Rusty in it. He'd become more attached to Rusty then he'd ever thought possible. He stood and moved to sit crosswise on Manny's lap. "That's at least a year and a half away. Plenty of time to figure it out."

Manny dropped the paper on the table before wrapping his arms around Adam's waist. "Are you sexually satisfied?"

Adam chuckled, surprised and confused by the question. "What?" He grinned. "Are you asking if you're enough man for me, because I thought we cleared that up years ago?"

"I meant with Rusty. I need to know that you're as invested in him as I'm quickly becoming," Manny explained.

"Are you still worried that Rusty and I don't fuck?" Adam made a face, hoping to convey his disappointment without saying the words. "Rusty gave me a blow job on the way to the mall. How could I possibly be anything other than satisfied with someone who'll go down on me anytime day or night." He reached down and rubbed the front of Manny's sweatpants. "Besides, you've been letting me fuck you more than you used to, so I'm good, babe." He tilted his head to the side. "What about you? Are you sexually satisfied?"

Manny stared into Adam's eyes, looking a little too serious for Adam's comfort. "I'm in love with him, *mi cielo*. There are times when I feel I can't breathe if he's not in my arms."

"That's good though, right?" Although they'd only been with Rusty for a little more than three weeks, Adam couldn't imagine his life without him.

"At semester break, I want to move him in," Manny declared.

"Okay," Adam readily agreed. "I'm actually surprised it's taken you this long to come to the realization that we need him with us permanently."

"I knew soon after we started seeing him, but I needed to know how you would handle the no fucking scenario before I said anything."

The statement hurt. Adam climbed off Manny's lap. "Do you really think I'm that shallow?"

Manny shook his head and reached for Adam, but Adam pulled away before he could connect. "I think it's harder for you to be around him and not fuck him than it is for me."

Adam carried his coffee to the sink and poured it out before reaching for an open bottle of wine in the refrigerator. He couldn't deny there had been times when he'd watched Manny finger Rusty's hole and wished he could thrust his cock inside that soft, tawny-colored pucker, but he'd dealt with it. "Does knowing I don't like to be rimmed make it too hard for you to be around me?"

"You know it doesn't, *mi cielo*."

Adam took a sip of his wine. "Well, there's your answer."

* * * *

Rusty sat in the back seat of Manny's sedan on the way to Will and Eric's. He could tell there was something going on between Manny and Adam by the way the two men refused to look at each other.

Usually, Manny drove with one hand on Adam's thigh as they laughed and sang along to the stereo, but that definitely wasn't the case. Rusty doubted Adam had taken his eyes off the view out of the passenger-side window, and Manny's hands were firmly on the steering wheel. He wanted to know what was going on, but he wasn't sure he had the right to ask. Still, the tension in the air was driving him nuts. "If you want to stop by a liquor store, I'll buy some wine," he offered.

Manny met Rusty's gaze in the rearview mirror. "I brought a couple of bottles from home for you, *bebé*."

"Thanks." Rusty made a mental note to restock the supply at the apartment.

By the time Manny parked in front of Will's house, Rusty couldn't get out of the car fast enough. He was so uneasy that he hurried to the house without waiting for Adam and Manny.

Eric answered the door. "Hey," he greeted.

"Hi." Rusty entered the house. He wished it was nice enough to sit outside on the patio, but unless they wanted to build a huge bonfire, they'd freeze their asses off. "Is Will in the kitchen?"

"Yeah. He's making another batch of fudge," Eric replied. "Hey, guys," he said when Manny and Adam entered the house.

Rusty tried not to look at either of his men. He knew rushing into the house had been a childish thing to do, but he wanted Manny and Adam to realize that he knew something was going on without him having to say it. "So are we going in there or staying in here?"

"We can start in the kitchen and move in here later." Eric closed the door and led the way into the kitchen.

Rusty started to follow but was pulled up short when Manny stepped in front of him. "What's wrong?" Manny asked.

"You tell me," Rusty replied. "It's obvious something's going on between you two."

"We're fine," Adam cut in. "We had a disagreement earlier, but it's over now."

"No it's not. You've barely spoken to each other all evening," Rusty pointed out.

"Manny, why don't you go in the kitchen while I talk to Rusty for a minute," Adam suggested.

Manny bent over and pressed his lips against Rusty's, sweeping his tongue inside for the briefest taste before pulling back. "Would you like a glass of wine?"

"Yes, thank you."

"I'll take one, too," Adam said, directing Rusty to the sofa.

Rusty settled on the couch. "What's going on?"

"We told you. We had a disagreement." Adam squeezed Rusty's hand. "Manny and I aren't perfect. We're a normal couple that argues on occasion. You'll understand in a few years. It's not something you need to worry about."

For some reason, the fact that Adam had used the word couple hurt. "I see." He didn't understand the sudden ache in his chest. He knew things were progressing nicely between the three of them, but with that single word, Rusty had been properly reminded that he was still an outsider. He'd also been reminded that he was much younger than Adam and Manny.

Rusty got to his feet and took a deep breath. He wondered if he'd ever be considered a member of Manny and Adam's family or if he'd forever be relegated to someone they were dating. *I've been so naïve. I can't believe I actually thought we were working toward a permanent arrangement.* His entire life, he'd wanted to be accepted and he'd stupidly thought he'd found what he'd always longed for. His eyes began to burn, but he refused to admit to Adam that his words had done more damage than a fist ever could. "All right then. I guess I'll leave the two of you alone about it." He walked away from Adam with his head held high and his heart breaking.

"Rusty."

Adam called after him, but Rusty didn't stop. As far as he could remember, his parents had only suffered one fight in their relationship. Unfortunately, Rusty had been home at the time, and the hateful way his mom and dad had spoken to each other was permanently etched into his psyche. Even after they'd made up and had forgotten the argument, Rusty hadn't been able to look at either of them the same again. He didn't want that, and he knew if he turned and confronted Adam, nothing good would come of it. He entered the kitchen just as Manny finished pouring four glasses of wine. "Thank you," he said, picking up the glass. *Please don't ask me*, he silently prayed. He tipped it back and drained the contents before holding it out for more.

Manny narrowed his eyes. He bent over and whispered in Rusty's ear, "Did Adam talk to you?"

"At me. To me. Same thing, right?" Rusty raised his glass and waited for Manny to fill it up again. His heart felt like it was breaking, and trying to hold himself together was getting harder by the minute.

Manny continued to stare at Rusty, making no move to pour the wine. "You should slow down," he admonished.

"Goddammit! I'm not a kid!" Rusty yelled, slamming the glass down on the counter. The impact shattered the delicate wineglass, cutting Rusty's hand in the process. "Sorry," he apologized to Will and Eric before marching out of the back door. Screw the cold. He'd much rather freeze to death outside than to spend another moment being treated like a child.

Rusty was heading to the gate at the side of the house when Manny called after him. "Stop!" he growled.

Rusty spun around. It wasn't often he got angry, but when he did, he didn't hold back. "Go back inside," he told Manny.

"Not without you, and not until you tell me what is wrong." Manny held out a dishtowel and gestured to Rusty's hand. "Do you need stitches?"

Rusty glanced at his hand. There was a small stream of blood running from the fleshy part between his thumb and index finger, but as he dabbed at it, he realized it wasn't as bad as it looked. "It's fine."

"Talk to me," Manny said, moving to stand in front of Rusty.

"In less than two minutes, I was reminded that you and Adam are a *couple*, and that maybe when I'm older I'll be able to understand that grownups argue sometimes," Rusty spat out, anger and hurt still coursing through his blood.

Manny glanced over his shoulder and it was then that Rusty noticed Adam standing just outside the backdoor. "Is that what happened?" Manny asked Adam.

"No," Adam replied. "I might have mentioned that we're a couple and couples argue sometimes, but I didn't say anything about Rusty getting older."

"You did, too," Rusty shot back. "You said maybe in a few years I'd be able to understand."

"Yes," Adam countered. "Because until a few minutes ago, I didn't foresee you getting into an argument with one of us in the near future. I *meant* that perhaps in a few years you would know that little arguments with one of us is to be expected. It had nothing to do with your fucking age, Rusty." Finished speaking, Adam stormed back into the house.

Rusty stared down at his hand and shook his head. Because he'd never dated, he wasn't sure how to deal with the situation. All he knew was that it hurt. He bit his bottom lip. "I suppose you think I acted like a child in there."

"I didn't say that."

"But you have to be thinking it," Rusty countered. His anger deflated as he exhaled a long breath. "Maybe I was. I didn't want to fight with Adam, so I ran, just like I've always done. My mom taught me that the safest thing to do when confronted was to run. I know she probably meant for me to get away from the bullies, but when Adam said those things, I felt like I used to right after I got knocked to the ground."

Manny wrapped his arms around Rusty. "If by using the term *couple*, Adam hurt your feelings, I can guarantee he didn't mean to. I know this is all new for you, but it's new for us, too." He kissed the top of Rusty's head. "Your parents didn't bicker, did they?"

"They got into an argument once, and it's something I'll never forget."

Manny chuckled. "My parents were very passionate people. They fought. They made-up. They loved. Perhaps it is hard for you to understand that having a quarrel does not mean an end of the love two people feel for each other."

"Will you tell me what the two of you argued about?" Rusty asked.

"No, but not for the reason you think. The three of us should sit down and discuss how we are going to handle disagreements. It's one thing if we're all arguing over something, but if one person is upset with something someone else did or said, I think it should stay between the two of them."

"Okay." It made sense to Rusty. "So I guess I should talk to Adam about how much it hurt when he excluded me."

"Yeah, but I have an idea he already knows." Manny released his hold on Rusty to cup his face in his big hands. "There's one more thing I need to tell you before you go inside."

"Okay." Rusty mentally prepared himself for what was coming next.

"*Te amo, bebé*," Manny whispered.

Rusty stared up at Manny. "You love me?"

"*Sí.*"

"I love you, too." Rusty pulled Manny's head down for a kiss. Before their lips touched, he whispered in return. "So much."

* * * *

Adam was sitting on the sofa, trying to make the best of a bad situation by talking to Will and Eric, when Rusty walked into the room. Cheeks pink from the cool temperature outside, Rusty strode straight to the couch and sat beside Adam.

"Sorry," Rusty said to Will and Eric, "but I need to apologize for overreacting to something Adam said to me earlier."

Eric chuckled. "No need to say you're sorry to us, you've heard the way Will and I go at it."

Rusty turned to face Adam. "I should've told you that what you said hurt my feelings instead of walking away the way I did."

"And I should have told you that people who love each other argue. Using the word couples was wrong." Adam slid his arm around Rusty and pulled him against his chest.

"Now that you've all made up, I'll take Rusty into the bathroom and get that cut cleaned up," Eric announced, getting to his feet.

Manny pushed away from the doorframe where he'd been standing, and moved to sit on the couch as Eric and Rusty left the room. "I told him how I feel," Manny told Adam.

Adam nodded.

Will chuckled and took a drink of his bourbon. "It's not as easy as you thought it'd be, is it?"

"Actually, except for a few small stumbling blocks, it's been an easier fit than I ever imagined," Adam answered truthfully.

"Good." Will rested his ankle on his knee. "However, I have to say, I've never heard Rusty use language like he did earlier. That your doing?"

Adam grinned, remembering. "Didn't get that from me. I think he's been hiding his light under a bushel for too long and he's finally breaking out of his shell."

"You may be right."

"Have there been any more attacks?" Manny asked.

"Nope. It's been quiet the last few weeks, which is good because we still don't have a clue who the jerks are. We've stepped up patrols at several of the clubs here in town. Maybe that's been enough to scare the pussies off." Will gestured to the plate of fudge on the coffee table. "Try some. It's my mom's recipe. I make it every year for the Thanksgiving potluck we have at the station."

Manny picked up a piece and popped it into his mouth. "Mmm," he groaned.

"Thought you'd like that," Will said, looking pleased with his culinary skills.

"You all have plans for Thanksgiving?" Will asked.

"We're staying home. It'll be Rusty's first Thanksgiving without his folks, so we thought it'd be best to have something quiet." Adam had hoped to see his mom and dad at some point during the holiday, but he and Manny had decided to see how Rusty did at Thanksgiving before they discussed Christmas plans. "Are you going to your parents' house?"

"Yep. We'll probably both be in a food coma by midday."

Adam watched as Manny ate another piece of fudge. He was about to ask Manny if they were okay when Manny reached down, grabbed another nugget and held it to Adam's mouth.

"You have to try this, *mi cielo*."

Adam wrinkled his nose. He'd never craved chocolate like most people, and except for the occasional candy bar, rarely ate the stuff.

"Try it," Manny urged, rubbing the fudge against Adam's lower lip.

Adam rolled his eyes and opened his mouth. The moment the fudge hit his tongue, it began to melt and damn the flavor was unbelievable. "Christ, Will, what the fuck're you doing wasting your talents as a detective? You should open a shop or something."

Will laughed. "Thanks, but I think I'll keep my day job."

* * * *

Rusty was chopping vegetables for the stuffing when Manny walked into the kitchen. "Is it on yet?"

Manny shook his head and stole a piece of celery. "Twenty minutes."

"Tell me again why you've decided to watch football?" Adam was peeling potatoes at the sink.

"Because it's Thanksgiving and that's what you're supposed to do on Thanksgiving," Rusty replied, wiping his hands on the apron Adam had insisted he wear while preparing food. Rusty assumed it had more to do with the fact that he'd been naked in the kitchen than Adam believing he was a messy cook.

"What should I do?" Manny asked.

"You can fill up the large stockpot with water for me," Adam suggested.

Manny reached up and grabbed the stockpot from the pot rack over the island before carrying it to the sink.

Rusty heard laughter and glanced over his shoulder to see Manny nipping at Adam's neck as the water ran. He was happy to see both his men were still in a good mood. The day had started out beautifully with a steamy session in bed where Manny had eaten his fill of strawberry flavored lube thanks to Rusty before proceeding to fuck a series of whimpers out of Adam.

Manny turned off the water. "Will you explain football rules to me?" he asked, moving to press himself against Rusty's back. He slid his hands under the apron and began to stroke Rusty's cock.

"Sorry. I don't really know the rules. Except a touchdown is worth six points and if they make that little kick thing afterward they get another point." Rusty put down the knife and leaned back against Manny. "The important thing is the noise of the crowd and watching all those men in tight pants."

Manny cupped Rusty's balls and gave them a gentle squeeze. "You're not really planning to watch the game are you?"

"No, but since I have to wait another two days for the next soccer game, I figured football would at least give you something to watch while we play."

Manny rubbed his erection against Rusty. "*Bebé*, I will play with your ass no matter what is on the television."

"No one's playing with asses until those vegetables are chopped and the dressing mixed up and put into the oven," Adam reminded them.

Rusty groaned. He wasn't used to helping in the preparation of Thanksgiving dinner, and when he'd agreed to help Adam, he'd had no idea Adam would be such a slave driver. "I know," he grumbled, turning back around. When he felt Manny's hand on his butt, Rusty waved the knife. "Probably not a good idea to distract me."

Manny chuckled and bit Rusty's bare shoulder before strolling out of the room.

"Does he ever help?" Rusty asked Adam.

"Never. Usually, we're at my parents' house, and I help Mom in the kitchen. Manny sits in front of the TV because according to him, Thanksgiving isn't a Spanish holiday."

Rusty wondered why Adam hadn't suggested going to his parents' house. "Can I ask you something?"

"Sure, as long as you keep cutting."

"Am I the reason you couldn't go home for Thanksgiving this year?" Rusty picked up the small cutting board and scraped the celery into the bowl of dried cubes of bread.

"No. It's not that we couldn't go to South Dakota. It's that we figured it would be easier for you if we stayed here this year. We know the holidays might be hard on you."

Rusty opened the can of chicken stock and poured it in the bowl before stirring. Several months earlier, he'd also worried that the holidays would be tough for him to get through, but even though he missed his mom and dad, he was handling it well. "I know where I want to scatter my parents' ashes," he blurted out.

Adam came up behind Rusty and took the long wooden spoon out of his hand before turning Rusty to face him. "Where, baby?"

Rusty felt his throat grow thick with emotion. "I don't know why I didn't think of it before, while I was still in Rutland." He met Adam's gaze. "They should end up where they started."

Adam's eyes filled with tears as he nodded. "The land?"

"Yeah." It has been three days since Rusty's lawyer had informed him that Virginia had agreed to drop the lawsuit if Rusty did the same with the countersuit. From the way it sounded, she'd wanted to push on, but her attorney had strongly advised against it. In the end, her own sense of self-preservation had finally kicked in.

"We can be on a plane first thing in the morning," Adam suggested.

Rusty thought about it for a few seconds before answering. "Thanks, but I think I'd rather go back in the spring. I'd like to plant a couple of trees, and November in Vermont is not a good time to do that."

"Okay. Whatever you want to do is fine. Just know that Manny and I will be there beside you."

"Game!" Manny yelled from the living room.

Adam gave Rusty a deep kiss. "Go on. I'll pour the stuffing into the pan and get it in the oven as soon as I pull the turkey out."

Rusty didn't immediately let go of Adam. Instead, he hugged him tighter. "If your parents are okay with me coming with you and Manny, I'd love to go home with you for Christmas."

"They'd love it."

The timer on the oven buzzed, prompting Rusty to pull away. "Yell if you need anything."

"I will," Adam said, pulling on his oven mitts.

Rusty untied his apron on the way to the living room. "You're not naked," he pointed out.

"No. We only have an hour before dinner. Better to save the naked stuff until after." Manny rubbed his palms against his jean-clad thighs. "This hour is for you."

Rusty straddled Manny's lap. "I gratefully accept your offer." He snuggled against Manny's chest right before kickoff.

Manny grabbed the bottle of lube and coated his fingers before moving down to circle Rusty's hole. "Are you doing okay today?"

"Yeah. I miss them." Rusty decided to open up to Manny and share with him the guilt he'd been feeling lately. "Sometimes, I think I'd give up everything to have them back, but then I realize that if they were still alive, I wouldn't be here with you and Adam."

"Adam's had his eye on your for years," Manny pointed out.

"Yeah, but without the accident, Eric would've never gone to get the two of you to help me deal with their death, and that was the first night Adam held me. I had a crush on him before, of course, but I'd have never taken it further than that until I actually felt his arms holding me. Then, when I saw the two of you together in Clean Slate that night, I knew a man like Adam would never give up a man like you for someone like me. I left early that night because I knew my heart couldn't take seeing the two of you so happy together. Then the attack happened."

Rusty felt Manny's entire body tense at the mention of the attack. He nuzzled his face against Manny's neck and smiled. He loved his overprotective man. "When you scooped me up into your arms that night, I'd never felt safer in my life." He lifted his head and gave Manny a quick kiss.

"Then you walked in on me and Adam," Manny remembered.

"Yeah. I was in bed and a loud thud woke me up. I started to worry that that guy who hit me had figured out where I was staying and had come for me. I heard it a few more times before I gathered my courage enough to go down the hall to your room. That's when I saw the two of you and realized the sound I kept hearing was Adam's back smacking against the window as you fucked him."

"I told Adam to shut the door that night, but he wanted it open. He wanted you to hear us because he wanted you to join us," Manny explained, pushing two of his fingers inside Rusty's hole.

"Part of me did want to join you, but I didn't know what to do, and I was afraid of making a fool of myself. The same thing with the time Adam propositioned me in the office. I was so torn because I wanted both of you, but I was so worried all you wanted from me was sex, and I'm not really made that way." Rusty sat up and rocked back and forth against Manny's skilled fingers.

"What made you change your mind?"

"I realized that my parents were gone, and unless I wanted to be alone the rest of my life, I needed to take a leap of faith and become the meat in the professor sandwich."

A bark of laughter erupted from Manny. "You are too cute, *bebé*."

"I'm glad I took a chance because I can't imagine my world without either of you." Rusty bit his lip. There was something else he needed to talk to Manny about, but he didn't want to hurt his feelings. "I think I need to ask Adam to fuck me," he admitted.

Manny's fingers stilled. "You don't have to do that."

"I know. You've both proven to me that I don't, but I think it bothers Adam that you've been inside of me but he hasn't. I think it's time." Before Manny could try to talk Rusty out of it, he yelled, "Adam! Can you come in here?"

Wiping his hands on a dishtowel, Adam entered the living room. "What? I'm not watching football."

"I need you to fuck me," Rusty said. Adam started to shake his head, but Rusty continued, "At least once, I want to know what it feels like to have you inside of me."

Adam straddled Manny's lap and pressed himself against Rusty's back. "I don't think I can fuck you, knowing you won't like it." He knocked Manny's hand away from Rusty's ass, and pushed two fingers deep into Rusty's hole. "I want to bring you pleasure in any way I can. Fucking is fantastic when both people want it, but I don't need it from you in order to love you. What the two of us share will always be enough for me. Do you understand?"

Rusty couldn't lie to either man. The only reason he'd wanted Adam to fuck him was because he'd started feeling guilty. It might seem like a strange analogy, but for him, fucking was like going to the dentist. It wasn't something he wanted to do, but it was something he felt he should do whether it was a pleasant experience or not. Knowing that Adam loved him regardless made him feel better. "Promise me something?"

"Anything," Adam replied, removing his fingers from Rusty's hole.

"If there ever comes a time when you need that from me, I want you to promise you'll tell me."

"I can do that." Adam leaned against Rusty and wrapped his arms around Manny as much as he could. "For the record," he whispered in Rusty's ear, "that turkey I felt up this morning has nothing on you."

Rusty chuckled. "Good to know."

BIG MAN ON CAMPUS

Dedication

Special hugs to my editor Sue, who said goodbye to
the love of her life recently.

Chapter One

Benny Allenbrand studied himself in the weight room mirror as he wiped the sweat from his face, neck and chest. At six-foot-seven, he'd always been big for his age, but playing college football would require more strength and agility than he'd needed on the Cattle Valley High School team. He'd taken a part-time job at The Gym, a local workout center, to help pay off a debt to his father. The fact that he could use the equipment before and after his shift was a bonus.

"Lookin' good." Rio Adega, The Gym's owner, began to unload the barbell Benny had used. "I have a feeling Coach Tucker's going to be impressed."

Nate 'Bear' Tucker was the offensive coach at North-Central Idaho University, and Benny's favorite player. Bear had been the shit when he'd played offensive lineman for the Bighorns, and Benny couldn't wait to make his coach proud.

"Thanks," Benny replied as he started toward one of the treadmills. "Bear will probably be surprised that I've grown another two inches since he first watched me play."

"You know it." Rio nodded his head toward the window. "I'm heading to the park to run. Why don't you come with me? You need to get used to the heat before practice starts, and I need to get outta here for a while."

Benny eyed his boss suspiciously. "You enjoy running by yourself. Why all of a sudden do you want my company?"

Rio's expression turned guilty. "Just thought you could use an ear. We all know it's not going to be easy for you and Chase to play on the same team. Figured you might want to talk to someone other than your dad about it."

Benny shook his head. "I haven't talked to Dad."

"What? I thought the two of you were tight." Rio headed for the door. "Be back in an hour," he told Kit, The Gym's manager.

"Wait right there." From her position behind the juice counter, Kit reached into the cooler. "It's hotter than Hades today." She removed two bottles of water before holding them out. "I need Benny to sanitize the mats later, so take it easy on him."

Rio winked and took the water. "He's eighteen. If he can't keep up with a man of my age, he doesn't deserve to call himself an athlete."

Kit crossed her arms over her ample chest and cocked her hip to the side but said nothing.

After several moments, Rio sighed. "Fine. I'll take it easy on the boy."

Benny snorted. He loved working at The Gym. Kit had been the first transgender person he'd ever met, but he'd soon forgotten the gorgeous woman had ever been anything but the lady she was.

"Be back with energy to spare," Benny told Kit.

"I'm counting on it!" she hollered as Benny and Rio walked out of the door.

As soon as they were outside, Benny started to stretch, but Rio shook his head. "Let's walk while you answer my question."

Benny groaned. "I don't want to talk about Chase."

It was bad enough that the entire town knew he'd lost his shit when Chase, his high school boyfriend, had broken up with him a few months before. The last thing he needed was to dissect his mistakes with his boss — one of the biggest badasses he'd ever known.

"Too bad," Rio said. "Because all the strength training in the world isn't going to help you on that field if your mind isn't in the game."

Benny walked several blocks without giving in to Rio's demands. What good would talking about Chase do? Chase had moved on to someone else even before he'd had the guts to break up with him.

"I could tell you there's someone else out there for you, but I doubt that would make you feel better," Rio said, breaking the silence.

Benny shook his head in agreement. He didn't dare confess that he'd spent the summer plotting revenge against the man who'd come between him and Chase or that, in his gut, he knew he was meant to be with Chase again. Instead of dreading the upcoming school year, he was looking forward to it because he knew he could prove to Chase how right they were together. He'd given the situation a lot of thought and it was obvious Chase had been lured away from him out of loneliness. It couldn't have been easy for Chase to move to a new city full of strangers. Chase probably been vulnerable when Mac Evans had swooped in to steal him away.

"You don't need to worry about that." Benny took a sip of water. "That thing between Chase and his new man won't last. You'll see. Once I'm on campus, Chase'll come back to me."

Rio stopped walking. "Benny…"

"Seriously. Don't worry." Benny glanced over his shoulder at Rio. "Come on, I've got to get this done so I can get back to work."

* * * *

Benny marked 'shower caddy' off his list before moving to the next item. "Bedding," he informed his dad, Brian. "XL twin sheets and a blanket or two. I thought I'd take my pillow with me."

Brian swung the shopping cart around and headed in the opposite direction. "You think you'll be able to sleep on a twin bed?"

Benny shrugged. "I guess I'll have to. I can't get a private room until I'm a junior, so until then, I'm going to have to share."

"You haven't slept in a bed that small since you were ten," Brian pointed out. He stopped at a display of *As Seen on TV* gadgets. "Maybe you should get one of these Ronco Ready Grills?"

Benny rolled his eyes and continued walking. His dad was notorious for buying shit off the TV that he never used. "All my meals are paid for."

"What if you need a snack or something in the evening?" Brian asked.

"Then I can go downstairs and see what's in the fridge." Benny looked back at his dad. "Seriously, do you think I'm going to need a grilled steak at ten o'clock at night?"

"You can grill something other than a steak," Brian mumbled as he set the box back down.

Benny turned his attention to the shelves of bedding. "What do you think about red sheets, or should I go with gray?"

"Unless you plan to change them more than you do now, I'd say stick to the dark gray. You can always get a red comforter," Brian suggested.

"Will going with the whole school color theme be too freshmany of me?" Benny asked.

"Freshmany?" Brian groaned. "You are taking at least one English class aren't you?"

"Only because it's required." Benny searched for and found a set of XL twin in dark gray. He refused to look at comforters because he always ended up kicking them off the bed anyway. Instead, he found a soft velour blanket in a deep red. It wasn't the exact shade of red the school used, so he figured he could get by with it. He tossed the items into the cart before pulling out his list again. "Done. All that's left is clothes."

Brian winced. "You'd have better luck taking Ethan with you for that."

As much as he liked his dad's partners, Ethan and Pete, he didn't think he needed anyone's help to pick out clothes. And, they were in Sheridan already, so it didn't make sense to drive all the way back to Cattle Valley to drop off his dad and pick up Ethan. "Why don't you just hang out at the food court while I get what I need?"

"Well, I guess I could do that, but I thought it would be a nice thing for you and Ethan to do together." Brian pushed the cart to the checkout line. "I'm not the only one who's going to miss you."

"Dad," Benny groaned. Adjusting to his dad's three-way relationship hadn't been easy, but he'd eventually come to terms with it. "Pete's already told me you bought season tickets to the games, so it's not like I'm never going to see you guys."

Benny felt eyes on them and turned to find an older woman staring at him. He wasn't sure if it was his size, the fact that he was a black man shopping in a home store or if the woman had overheard too much of their conversation. He narrowed his gaze and stared down at her as if she were an offensive lineman he wanted to eat for dinner.

The woman made a startled noise before pushing her cart to a different line.

Satisfied, Benny grinned at his dad. "Working out all the time definitely has advantages."

Brian chuckled and shook his head. "Boy, that shit's gonna get you in trouble one day."

"Maybe, but I'll use it to my advantage until that day comes," Benny replied.

* * * *

Everett James Whitmore III pulled another suitcase out of his closet. He wasn't supposed to return to school for another month, but between his mother's hovering and his father's demands, Jamie had to get away. Without his father's money, he'd need to visit the admissions office, find a place to live and talk to Professor Willis about switching his major, and that would take time.

A soft knock on his bedroom door drew his attention. He had no doubt it was his mother trying to get him to see reason—or at least his father's version of it.

"Come in," he called without looking away from his task.

"Lunch is ready," his mother said as she opened the door. "What're you doing?"

"Leaving." Jamie glanced over his shoulder. He loved his mother, but, whether it was the society Stephanie Cryer-Whitmore had been born into or the years of living under Senator Everett James Whitmore II's thumb, she hadn't stood up for him when he'd finally come out to his father.

"What?" She pressed a manicured hand to her chest. "You can't leave. Your father's invited the Jenkinses for dinner."

Jamie turned away from his mom to grab another handful of T-shirts from his drawer. Allan Jenkins was a congressional representative from their home state of Connecticut who just happened to have an attractive daughter a few years younger than Jamie. "Sorry, Mother, but Clarisse Jenkins isn't going to turn me straight." He pulled out his sock drawer and dumped the contents into the suitcase. "After the scene yesterday, I think it's better I just get out of here."

"Jamie." His mother moved to sit on the black leather bench at the foot of Jamie's massive bed. "I think you're being too hard on your father. He's simply trying to make the best out of a public relations nightmare."

Jamie stilled at the statement. "This isn't a PR nightmare, Mother, this is my life!"

She reared back as if Jamie had slapped her. "Where is this coming from? You weren't raised like this."

Jamie took several calming breaths before moving to sit beside his mother. He reached for her hand. "I love you, but I won't be Father's gay poster boy to get sympathy votes from other Republicans, and I absolutely refuse to exploit my sexual preference in front of the cameras to get him the LGBT vote in November."

"You don't understand, Jamie. If we don't make a public announcement about you, your father's opponent will dig the information up and use the dirt against him. I didn't raise you to be this selfish," she scolded.

Jamie shook his head. "That's the point. I'm not dirt to be used against — or for — anyone. I'm your son. I've lied to everyone around me for years because you convinced me that someday I could live my own life. I'm twenty-one. At what age does my happiness start to matter to you?"

She squeezed Jamie's hand before getting to her feet and smoothing her coiffed, dark brown hair. "If you refuse to spin the situation the way your father has asked, we can address this subject again after the November election."

"That's what you said when I wanted to tell him after my eighteenth birthday," Jamie argued. He looked around his room. "I'm sorry. I can't do it anymore. I just can't." He zipped his suitcase and set it next to the others he'd already packed. "I'm taking my car to school, but if Father insists on taking it back, I'll text you the location."

"Don't do this, Jamie. You know what your father's like when he feels cornered. You only have one year left before you can transfer to the Masters' program at Georgetown. That was our deal when we allowed you to go to that no-name college in Idaho. You know it wasn't easy for him to capitulate on your choice, but you promised to end your college career at Georgetown."

"I'm changing majors," he announced. "You and I both know I'm not cut out for a career in politics. I hate everything about it."

Her artfully made-up eyes rounded in surprise. "You're going into your senior year. What other career do you hope to slip into?"

Jamie licked his lips. Since his freshman year, he'd used his own money to pay for independent ceramics classes taught by Daniel Willis, who, in Jamie's opinion, was one of the best artisans he'd ever met. "I still have to talk to my advisor, but I hope to have enough credits to graduate with a fine arts degree with an emphasis in ceramics and pottery."

He held his breath and waited for the explosion.

"Why would you do that to us? We've always indulged your hobby despite the message it sends to our friends. Is this your way of getting back at us?" she asked.

"It's not just a hobby, Mother, it's a passion, and one that I'm damn good at." He walked over to his dresser and picked up a vase he'd finished before leaving school. The delicate cherry blossoms he'd cut into the clay's surface before firing had taken him nearly three weeks to accomplish but that was only because his time had been limited due to hours spent on classes he'd cared nothing about.

He handed the vase to his mother. "This piece will outlive us both. I'd rather be remembered for creating works of beauty than being a lobbyist for some corporation I care nothing about."

She studied the art piece for several moments before holding it out. "It's pretty, but it serves no purpose. Whereas you can make a real difference in Washington if you put your mind to it, and make enough money to own a home like this one someday."

She waved her hand at the vase. "All that'll get you is a one-bedroom apartment in a rundown building. You're better than that, Jamie."

Jamie gave up. "Sorry, Mother, but I've made my choice."

"How're you going to pay for college if your father cuts you off?" Stephanie asked.

"I have money," Jamie reminded her. "I'll have to make a few changes, but it's enough to pay for the rest of my school and get me started after graduation." Surprisingly, when it came down to it, it had been an easy decision to walk away from his father's money. He took a deep breath and realized that for the first time in years, he felt free...free to follow his own career path, free to enjoy the art he'd always been forced to hide away, and free to love someone of his own choosing.

Feeling better, Jamie kissed his mother's cheek. "I'll call you as soon as I find a place to live."

He didn't dare tell his parents he was planning to beg for a room at BK House, the gay men's private dormitory on campus. Luckily, his ceramics professor's partner, Tony Bianchi, was not only a millionaire, but he was also a major benefactor of BK House.

"You're making a mistake," she told him as he followed her out of the bedroom with his first load of luggage.

"My only mistake was to believe you'd eventually put my happiness before Father's political aspirations."

* * * *

Jamie knocked on the closed door of Professor Willis' studio. He'd called earlier and Daniel had told

Jamie that he would be at the college most of the day, which was a real break for Jamie.

The small camera over the door made a whirring sound as it zoomed in. Jamie smiled up and waved to his professor. From what Jamie had been told, a psycho ex had terrorized Daniel in the past, so Daniel's partner had insisted on upgraded security when Daniel worked alone.

The door's lock disengaged and it swung open to reveal the good-natured professor. "Jamie!" Professor Willis threw his arms around Jamie and gave him a brief hug before stepping out of the doorway. He gave Jamie's shoulder-length hair a playful flick. "Love it."

Jamie ran a hand through his dark hair. Forgoing haircuts for the previous six months had been his first act of rebellion. "It's been hard to get used to, but it's finally long enough to put back when I need to."

"Come in and tell me what's going on."

Jamie had phoned Professor Willis on the long drive from Washington DC to inform him of his plan to switch majors, but the two of them hadn't gotten into the particulars. Jamie glanced around the room. "No summer classes?"

Daniel shook his head. "Tony and I spent six weeks in Europe. I figured if he could take time off work, so could I." He led Jamie to a clean worktable. After sitting on one of the stools, he gestured for Jamie to do the same. "So tell me what happened?"

"How do you know something happened?" Jamie asked.

"Because I've tried to steal you away from the political science department since you were a freshman to no avail and suddenly you're ready to jump ship before your senior year."

Because Jamie needed Daniel's help, he knew he had to be honest. "I came out to my father." He thought of the cruel words his father had lobbed at him. "Needless to say, he wasn't happy. He actually told me I was dead to him, but then he spoke to his campaign manager and the two of them came up with a plan to use my 'deviant behavior' to his own advantage," he said, using air quotes to make his point.

"Shit," Daniel muttered.

"Yeah. I told him I wasn't about to beg my fellow 'queers' in Connecticut for their votes for my devoted father." Jamie still couldn't believe his father'd had the nerve to ask such a thing of him, especially after the variety of derogatory names he'd shouted at the top of his lungs. "Unfortunately, he didn't believe me, merely reminded me who was paying my way through school." He shrugged. "After I'd had time to give it thought, I decided to start living the life I've always wanted, so here I am."

"Even if you take pottery classes full-time, I'm not sure you'll have enough to graduate this year," Daniel pointed out.

"Maybe not. That's something else I wanted to discuss with you. I'll need a new advisor," Jamie said.

Daniel tapped his forefinger against his lips for several moments before speaking. "I don't normally advise students, but if I can get it cleared through the department head, I'll do my best to make sure you graduate in time."

"Graduation doesn't mean as much to me as learning the skills to succeed," Jamie replied.

Daniel shook his head. "You're one of the most naturally gifted students I've ever had the pleasure to work with. I can show you new techniques, but you already possess the skills to succeed. Why do you think I've been on your ass since freshman year when you wandered in and asked if you could take an independent study class with me?"

Jamie remembered how nervous he'd been. He'd taken a pottery class his sophomore year of high school because he'd needed a fine arts requirement to graduate, and he'd figured throwing clay around would be an easy A. Little had he known he would take to it so completely. He'd managed to work four more courses into his schedule before he'd graduated, but when he'd originally set his college schedule, he hadn't been able to convince his father that a class in ceramics would be beneficial. Finally, his sophomore year, he'd gathered the courage to approach Professor Willis.

"I have another favor to ask. I'm getting ready to head over to BK House to see if they have a spot for me." Jamie stood before shoving his hands in his front pockets. "I thought maybe you could put in a good word for me?"

"What about your place in the Arlington Building?" Daniel asked.

"My father pays for that apartment, and since I've burned that bridge, I'm going to need something a lot less expensive."

Without hesitation, Daniel pulled out his phone, hit a few buttons and put it to his ear. "Hey, Charlie, it's Daniel. Are you busy?"

Jamie listened closely to Daniel's side of the conversation.

"Preaching to the choir." Daniel laughed. "Yeah. Hey, are there any beds left for the upcoming year? I've got a student in need." His expression fell. "When will you know for sure?" He blew out a breath and glanced at Jamie. "Okay. I'll have him come by and fill out an application."

From the sounds of it, Jamie would have to make a trip to the housing office to see if he could get a room in one of the dormitories. It sucked, but he couldn't expect to get everything he'd wanted.

"No, really. It's okay. I'll take care of it for now," Daniel said, before hanging up.

"No go?" Jamie asked, already knowing the answer.

"Not right now, but Charlie said there are always one or two who chicken out and don't show up. In the meantime, you're welcome to stay in the pool house at our place."

Jamie couldn't believe his instructor had made such a grand offer. He'd seen the mansion Tony and Daniel called home and although it was pure luxury, he knew how private the couple were. "Thanks, but I couldn't intrude."

Daniel chuckled. "You won't be intruding. Tony's away at a convention in Buenos Aires until late next week anyway. You'd be doing me a favor, since I hate to be alone."

Jamie didn't buy the professor's line of bullshit, but he found himself nodding. "Okay. I'd appreciate it. I'll also fill out an application for the regular dorms on campus. Hopefully, I'll be able to find someplace to live before the semester starts."

Daniel waved his hand. "Don't worry about it. The pool house is empty anyway. You can crash there as long as you need to. Charlie said dropouts are also common, so they'll likely find a place for you in the next month or two." He clapped his hands before rubbing them together. "This could be fun. I'm a lot older than you are, but there are so many things I haven't done, and a sleepover with a friend is one of them."

"Uhhh, maybe you should talk to Mr. Bianchi first. He may not like the idea of another man staying at your house while he's away, and I like my face the way it is," Jamie replied.

"Don't call him Mr. Bianchi." Daniel smiled. "It'll give him a bigger head than he's already got, and don't worry about staying over. He'll be thrilled I have someone else there."

Skeptical, Jamie rubbed the back of his neck. "I'd still feel better if you called him."

"Fine." Daniel punched more buttons on his phone before putting it on speaker.

"Hey, babe," Tony answered. "You need me to talk dirty to you again already?"

"Yes, but that's not why I'm calling. You're on speaker with me and Jamie Whitmore."

"Hey, Jamie," Tony greeted, sounding as if he didn't mind Jamie overhearing his earlier remark.

"Hi, Tony," Jamie returned.

"Listen, Jamie needs a place to crash for a while until BK has an opening. I told him he could stay in the pool house. Is that cool with you?" Daniel asked.

"Sure," Tony replied with enthusiasm. "Actually, I'll feel a lot better if you have someone there while I'm gone."

"That's what I told him, but he was afraid you'd break his face," Daniel relayed.

Tony laughed for several seconds. "I don't make a habit of breaking faces unless I have just cause. The only thing I ask of you is to remind Daniel to put the garbage cans out on Thursday morning before eight."

Although Jamie had met Tony on a few occasions, he'd always felt intimidated by Tony's power and wealth, but he was quickly figuring out the rich businessman wasn't anything like he'd assumed. "I'll take care of the trash," he offered. "It's the least I can do."

"See? Jamie's paying for his keep already." Daniel slapped Jamie on the shoulder. "Do you do dishes?"

"Don't start pawning all your chores off on Jamie," Tony growled without any heat behind his words.

"I do know how to wash dishes, so we can trade off that duty," Jamie said.

"Are you going to need another wheel for the shop?" Tony asked.

Daniel's face lit up at the suggestion. "Yes! Would you mind if I set up a whole other station for Jamie? That way he can work alongside me and Rocco."

"You can do anything you want, babe. Just put it on the card."

"Have I told you today how much I love you?" Daniel asked Tony.

"Yep, but I can never hear it enough. I've got to go, babe, but I'll call you later, after my meetings."

"Okay. Talk to you later." Daniel made kissy noises into the phone.

"Thank you, Tony," Jamie said before Daniel could hang up.

"No need for that. Just keep Daniel occupied when I'm not around, and we'll be square."

Jamie felt lighter than he had in years. "I can do that."

Chapter Two

Benny parked in front of BK House and stared up at his new home for the next four years. "Well, this is it."

"It's bigger than I thought it'd be," Brian said as he slid out of the passenger seat.

Pete's brand new black pickup backed into the space closest to the front door of the three-story building. Benny groaned when Ethan climbed out of the truck and into Brian's arms. It wasn't like the sight of his father kissing either Pete or Ethan was uncommon, but did they have to do it in front of the dorm?

"Dad," Benny whined after he'd unfolded himself from his car. "You just did that two hours ago when we stopped for lunch."

Pete chuckled. "Ethan's a great kisser. I don't blame him. As a matter of fact..." His voice trailed off as he took his turn at Ethan's mouth.

"Fuck my life," Benny muttered as he popped the trunk.

"You need some help?"

Benny glanced up to find Locky, the man in charge of new residents, standing at the top of the steps with his arm slung over the shoulder of a younger man with black hair. He'd met Locky when he'd attended one of Chase's football games, but the other guy didn't look familiar. "Thanks, but if I can get them to let each other go long enough to help, we should be able to take care of it in a few trips."

Brian climbed the steps and held out his hand. "Hi. I'm, Brian Allenbrand, Benny's dad."

"Lockwood Regent, but everyone calls me Locky." He bumped his hip against the man standing next to him. "This is my partner Becket." He gestured to the ratty T-shirt and jean shorts they were both wearing. "Becket offered to help me paint today, so I've put him to work."

Brian pointed at Ethan and Pete, who had thankfully stopped kissing. "Those are my partners, Ethan and Pete."

Benny left the boxes in the trunk and, instead, decided to get his new thirty-two inch TV out of the backseat before joining his dad, Becket and Locky on the steps.

"You're on the third floor, room three twelve," Locky informed him. "Becket'll show you. I'll grab a box."

Benny waited for Becket to open the door before he entered the house. "You go to school here?"

"I did. I graduated last year." Becket led the way up the staircase. "BK's a cool place to live, and Jack's a great cook, but run if creamed tuna's on the menu."

"I heard that," a deep voice said from the living room below.

"Jack?" Benny whispered to Becket.

Becket nodded. "It's a running joke around here. Jack decided to give us a taste of life in the military one night and served creamed tuna on toast." He shook his head. "Nastiest stuff I've ever put in my mouth."

Benny continued up from the second floor to the third. He wasn't sure how to cream tuna, but it didn't sound good. He followed Becket down the hall. "Is my roommate here yet?"

"Nope. Locky tries to put the athletes in with the bookworms. Might sound crazy, but it seems to work because the geeks like quiet time to study and since the jocks spend most of their time at the athletic center it's the perfect combination." Becket opened the door to three twelve. "This is it."

Benny carried the television into his new room. He glanced around for somewhere to sit the screen. "That desk mine?"

Becket nodded. "Yeah, but if you put that there, where're you going to study?"

"At home, I did it at the kitchen table. I've tried doing it in my room, but if I'm already tired and the bed's right there, homework is the last thing I'll want to do." Benny steadied the TV on the small desk. "That'll work."

Becket stared up at Benny. "You're huge. I think you might even be bigger than Bear."

Benny was pleased someone had noticed but didn't confirm Becket's assessment. He stared down at the extra-long twin. "My dad's worried about the bed. I thought he was nuts, but now that I look at it..." He glanced at Becket. "I'm in trouble, right?"

Becket bit his bottom lip. "Depends. Do you move when you sleep?"

"Yeah, usually, but I've had a king since my tenth birthday."

Brian whistled when he walked into the room. "That's a long haul." Pete, Ethan and Locky closely followed him. "Where do you want these?" his dad asked.

With so many people in the room, Benny had no idea. "Put 'em on my roommate's side until I can unpack."

"That'll work," Locky said. "Ira's not due to arrive until sometime next weekend."

"Umm, Benny?" Ethan prompted.

Benny turned to look at the smaller of his dad's partners. "Yeah?"

"Will you do me a huge favor? Just once, I'd like to see you lie on that bed." Ethan clasped his hands together as if he were about to pray. "Please?"

Benny wanted to tell Ethan to fuck off, but he couldn't with his dad in the same room. "Tell ya what, you bring up the rest of the stuff, and I'll do just that."

"Benny," Brian said in warning.

"Fine." Truth be told, Benny also wondered how in the hell he was supposed to spend every night in the tiny bed. He sat in the center of the mattress before swinging his legs up as he lowered his torso. *Shit.* In order to give himself enough headroom, his feet hung off the bottom of the bed. Unfortunately, the biggest problem was the width of his shoulders. No way in hell he'd be able to move an inch without falling out of bed.

"Big man in a little bed," Ethan sang, changing the words to his favorite Chris Farley movie line.

Benny had already known it was coming so he just rolled his eyes. "Laugh it up, shrimp. You'd probably get lost in this bed."

Ethan elbowed Brian. "Did you hear that?"

Brian chuckled. "Yeah. Good one, Ben."

With a groan, Benny sat up. "Let's get this done." As much as he loved his dad, Ethan and Pete, he was ready for a break. Besides, he wanted to go to Clean Slate and see if Chase still worked there.

* * * *

Jamie was on the way out of his temporary home when his phone rang. One look at the display and he cringed. He'd put off talking to his parents for three days, and the calls were becoming more frequent. Resigned to the fact that he couldn't avoid his father's wrath much longer, he put the phone to his ear and stared out at the pool. Instead of stark concrete, Tony had designed the area to resemble the Garden of Eden—complete with a waterfall and lined with natural river rock. "Hello?"

"Nice of you to finally answer," Everett, Jamie's father, replied.

"I've been busy." Jamie locked the pool house. "So, if you're calling to see if I've changed my mind, I haven't."

"I spoke with the building manager and he said you haven't been to the condo."

"He's right. I told Mother I wasn't staying there because I knew you'd just use it to control me. Same with everything else. If you want the Audi, just let me know and I'll give you an address where you can pick it up."

"You're being childish," Everett barked. "All I've asked of you is to accompany me to a few rallies to talk to your peers."

Jamie groaned. It was the same conversation they'd had several days earlier. "And say what? That you support gays? I can't do that because we both know that's a damn lie. You don't even support me, and I'm your son."

"I don't have time for this. One of my sources told me Ed Rogan's team received a tip that you were spotted in a gay bar in Baltimore while home for the summer. According to my inside guy, Rogan even has a picture of you and another man *dancing*. He's planning to leak the information to the press any day. My whole staff is working on damage control, but as far as I'm concerned, this is your mess to clean up and the way to do that is to join my campaign."

"You coming?" Daniel yelled as he exited the main house.

Jamie held up a finger before returning his attention to his father. "You know what, why don't you just go on record with the truth? You have a gay son that you're ashamed of. I'm sure you'll get every homophobic vote in Connecticut."

"If I had my way, I'd do just that. Unfortunately, my own state has been overrun with deviants like you. According to my staff, I have to play nice with the queers, and that means making peace with you long enough to win the election."

"Sorry to disappoint you, *Dad*, but I'm not interested." Jamie hung up the phone before his asshole father could say another word. Jamie growled his frustration at the top of his lungs.

Daniel, who had disappeared around the corner of the house, came running back to the pool area. "What happened?"

Jamie stared at Daniel. He'd never seen his laid-back professor look so panicked. "Sorry. Shit, I'm so sorry I worried you." He held up the phone. "Just my dad."

Daniel visibly relaxed and dropped to one of the patio chairs and pressed a hand to his chest. "Christ. You scared the shit out of me."

Jamie assumed Daniel's reaction had something to do with Tony's security concerns, but he'd never been given specifics, and he wasn't about to ask. "Sorry," he said again.

"You want to talk about it?" Daniel asked.

What Jamie really needed was a drink. "Not really, but I'll buy you a Jack and Coke at Clean Slate, if you're interested, and we can take it from there."

Daniel pulled out his phone. "Sure. I'll call Rocco and tell him we'll meet him another night."

Jamie had been looking forward to getting to know Rocco Williams. They'd met on a few occasions, but Jamie had been too star-struck by the well-known artist to say more than one or two awkward words. "Why don't you ask him to join us?"

Daniel studied Jamie for a moment. "You sure?"

"Yeah. From what my father told me, everyone will know my story in the next few days anyway." Although the upcoming election in Connecticut shouldn't be national news, Everett Whitmore II was widely known as a staunch conservative who consistently voted against liberal issues. The discovery of Jamie's homosexuality would be a scandal too good for the media to ignore.

Fuck.

* * * *

After promising his dad that he'd meet him, Pete and Ethan for breakfast the next morning, Benny took a quick shower and was out of the door. He'd looked up the address to Clean Slate on his phone and was pleased to see it wasn't that far from the dorm.

By the time he'd reached the club, he'd psyched himself up for his first encounter with Chase. If everything went his way, his ex would take one look at his sculpted body and drop the old man he'd been living with. He glanced down at the white, short-sleeve Under Armour compression shirt and grinned. The shirt showed every muscle in his torso to perfection. No way could Chase not notice the changes in his body. Teamed with his favorite pair of tattered but stylish jeans, he knew he looked good.

Benny was surprised to find a bouncer checking identification at the door to the club. He knew he looked much older than his eighteen years, so he decided to play it cool and hope the big guy let him through the door.

"ID," the bouncer said, holding out his hand.

Fuck. Benny pulled out his wallet and handed over his driver's license. "A friend of mine works here. I thought I'd stop in for a burger or something and say hi."

"What's his name?" the bouncer asked.

"Chase." Benny shrugged. "We went to high school together."

The bouncer handed Benny's license back before grabbing a bright orange paper wristband. "You're in luck. Chase is filling in for one of the regular servers tonight. You'll have to wear this."

Under 21 was printed on the bracelet, but Benny didn't care as long as it got him into the place. He held out his arm.

The bouncer chuckled. "You're a big boy. I think I'm going to have to stick two of these together or risk cutting off your circulation."

"Whatever works," Benny replied.

Once he'd been dutifully identified as underage, Benny was allowed to enter the bar. He slipped into a booth as he scanned the crowd for the blond-haired, blue-eyed man he loved. The moment he spotted Chase, his mouth went dry. Chase looked better than he ever had — something Benny chalked up to age and the fact that Chase loved his job. He refused to consider the wide smile on Chase's face could have anything to do with Mac, the man who had taken Chase away from Benny. He lifted his hand in an attempt to get Chase's attention.

The smile on Chase's face died the moment his gaze landed on Benny. He said something to one of the bartenders before heading Benny's way. By the time he reached Benny, he'd regained his smile but it didn't look the same as before.

"Hey," Chase greeted. "When did you get into town?"

"Today," Benny replied. He gestured to the bench seat across from him. "Do you have time to sit?"

Chase glanced over his shoulder at the room. "Sorry, but we're pretty jammed, and I'm the only server on duty. Actually, I can't believe you even caught me here. I quit several months ago and started working at Mac's dealership, but the owner of this place asked me to fill in for a few weeks until he could hire more people."

"I just want a chance to talk to you." Benny smoothed his hand down the front of his shirt. He hoped it looked like a casual gesture, but he was really hoping Chase would notice his body and change his mind.

"Tonight's not good for me. I can take your order, but I don't have time to get into a discussion with you. Practice starts Monday. Maybe we can get together one day next week."

"Are you kidding me? We haven't spoken since March." Benny clenched his hands under the table in an attempt to get his rising anger under control. The last time he'd seen Chase, he'd lost his shit and had trashed Mac's pickup in retaliation. It hadn't been his finest moment, but it had been real.

"I'm sorry, Benny, but I have customers." Chase licked his lips. "Did you want to order something?"

Benny wasn't ready to give up. "Yeah, get me a double cheeseburger, fries and a Coke."

"Do you still eat your burger medium rare?" Chase asked.

Benny nodded. "You remembered."

Chase's expression softened. "Of course I remember." He sighed. "I'll never forget our time together, and I still hope we can be friends, but that's all it can ever be."

"I don't believe you," Benny said. "We're meant to be together, and we both know it."

Chase shook his head. "You can stay for dinner, but then it would probably be best if you leave. Mac'll be in after he closes the shop, and the last thing in the world I need is for the two of you to get into it."

Benny knew it was time to back off or risk alienating Chase on his first day in town. He held up his hands in the universal sign of surrender. "I promise not to beat the crap out of your old man."

Chase walked off without another word, leaving Benny to watch Chase's perfect ass as it disappeared in the crowd. Benny doubted Chase would've acted so angry if he didn't still have feelings for him. Yeah, he could play it cool for a few days until he got another chance to talk to the man he loved.

* * * *

Jamie took another sip of his drink, only half-listening to Rocco talk about his latest show. His attention had been riveted to the black man four tables away since the moment he'd walked into the club. *Holy fuck.* He wasn't used to being the aggressor, but he couldn't let the moment pass without acknowledging his unusual attraction to the guy. He'd just gotten to his feet when the cute blond server approached the god's table.

Jamie sank back down in his seat, intending to wait until the blond had taken the man's order. Unfortunately, the men appeared to know each other, and from the black man's body language, the conversation wasn't making him happy.

"Earth to Jamie," Daniel said, elbowing Jamie in the ribs. "Something strike your fancy?"

Jamie nodded toward the booth and the man who had so captured his attention. "I think I'm in lust. Jesus, have you ever seen anyone so fucking beautiful?"

Daniel cleared his throat. "Yeah," he answered with an indignant tone. "I happen to live with the most beautiful man in the world."

"That's gotta be Benny Allenbrand. Bear hasn't stopped talking about his star recruit from Cattle Valley," Rocco said. "From the size of that man, it has to be him." He winked at Jamie. "And, you're in luck because he claimed a spot at BK House, which means he's like-minded."

Benny. Jamie rolled the name around in his head. "He doesn't look like a Benny."

Rocco and Daniel both chuckled. "Yeah," Rocco began, "don't get used to it. Bear's famous for giving his players nicknames."

"Who's that he's talking to?" Jamie asked.

"Chase Hughes. The team's quarterback. He's also from Cattle Valley," Rocco said.

"Why all of a sudden do you know so much about the players?" Daniel emptied his beer mug before wiping his mouth.

Rocco snorted. "I live with an ex-football player who's obsessed with the Bighorns. I swear, the older Joe gets, the more he clings to his glory days on the field."

Jamie cared nothing about football, but watching Benny play may just be the motivation he'd needed to get into the sport.

When Chase walked away from Benny's table, it was obvious to Jamie that the conversation hadn't gone well. "I was going to go talk to him, but his body language is screaming keep away."

"Hell yeah it is," Daniel agreed. "Maybe we should have a BK House pool party? We've had them before, so it won't be too obvious."

Jamie liked the idea of seeing Benny in a pair of swim trunks. "I'm in," he announced.

Daniel pulled out his phone. Without his normal cooing to Tony, he launched into his plan. "So, listen, I want to host a back-to-school party for BK House. Jamie's gaga over the new football star in town who just happens to live at BK."

Jamie returned his attention to Benny and was flabbergasted to find the gorgeous hunk staring straight at him. Jamie chanced a slight smile to let Benny know he was open to an approach, but instead of smiling back, Benny broke eye contact and turned his head toward the bar.

Jamie glanced in the direction of Benny's gaze and sighed when he saw Chase loading a tray of drinks.

"Is there something between the two of them?" he asked Rocco.

"I don't know. Want me to find out?" Rocco asked.

"Yeah." As attracted as he was to Benny, the last thing he wanted was to fall for someone who was already taken.

In no time, Rocco had his phone pressed to his ear. "Hey, what's the story with Benny and Chase?"

Jamie glanced at Daniel, who was still on the phone discussing details with Tony, before turning his attention back to Rocco.

Rocco nodded several times. "No shit. Yeah, I know him. He's a great guy." Rocco nodded again. "All right. Thanks, Bear. No, Benny hasn't done anything, I've got a friend who was wondering if he was single. That's all." He looked at Jamie. "Sure. I'll tell him. Bye." He hung up and scooted even closer to Jamie.

"What?" Jamie asked, leaning toward Rocco.

"Well, according to Bear, Chase and Benny used to date. Guess they were high school sweethearts. Chase is a few years older than Benny, and up until four months ago, seemed perfectly loyal to Benny. That is until Chase met Mac, a local Harley dealer. I guess Mac and Chase hit it off and Chase broke it off with Benny. Evidently Benny didn't take it well and trashed Mac's truck when Chase went home to Cattle Valley to talk to Benny about it."

"Fuck," Jamie muttered.

"Yeah. There wasn't a police report filed because Mac refused to press charges, but Benny called Bear and confessed his part in the crime anyway. Bear's got mad respect for the dude to owning up to his mistake, but he's also keeping an eye on Benny to make sure his temper doesn't get the better of him again." Rocco glanced at Benny. "You sure you still want him?"

Jamie leaned his chin on his hand. "Not sure. I'll let you know after Daniel's party."

Chapter Three

Impressed by the natural look of the pool and its surroundings, Benny dropped his towel on one of the lounge chairs before going in search of something to drink. In his current mood, he wasn't sure why he'd agreed to come to the party, except to get Locky and Becket off his back, and the fact that he hoped Chase would attend. Other than a few guys he'd seen around the dorm, he didn't know any of the twenty or so guests.

"Well, hey there," a small blond man with long hair greeted him as he stepped up to the bar. "I'm Daniel." He pointed to a good-looking older man who stood in front of a massive grill. "And that's my partner Tony."

Benny recognized from their names that they were the hosts of the party. "Nice to meet you." He pointed toward his chest. "I'm Benny."

"What can I get you to drink, Benny? Sorry, no alcohol for anyone underage."

"Doesn't matter. I'll take a bottle of water if you've got it." A man carrying a tray of food caught his attention. It was the same man he'd noticed at the club the previous week.

"That's Jamie," Daniel provided without Benny asking. "He's staying in our pool house until a room at BK opens up."

"He a transfer?" Benny asked, because no way was the guy a freshman.

"Nope, but his situation changed at the last minute so he's on the waiting list." Daniel handed Benny a bottle. "Once I've met everyone, I'll set a big tub of water and soft drinks by the food table, but I've found this is the best way to get to know the new residents."

"Good idea." Benny unscrewed the cap. "Did you invite Chase Hughes?" Chase had dodged him after practice for an entire week, and Benny was starting to lose patience.

"No," Daniel replied. "We decided to stick with close friends and the guys of BK House that came into town early."

"Get out! I told you I had nothing to say to you!" someone screamed, drawing Benny's attention.

"Shit." Daniel came out from behind the bar. "Tony!"

"What's going on?" Benny asked, setting his bottle down.

Daniel shook his head. "Reporters. Jamie's going through some personal stuff. We thought this might happen, but we'd hoped they wouldn't figure out where he was living."

"I've got it, babe," Tony said as he rushed by Daniel.

"Does he need help?" Benny asked. He wasn't doing anything anyway. Might as well use his size for something other than football.

"Would you mind?" Daniel asked, looking imploringly up at Benny. "If nothing else, get Jamie away from them before he says something he'll regret."

"Right." Benny handed Daniel his water before taking off in the same direction Tony had gone. He unlatched the tall privacy fence and spotted Tony trying to put himself between Jamie and a reporter.

"How long has your father known about your homosexuality?" the correspondent asked shoving the microphone toward Jamie.

Tony pushed the man hard enough for him to lose his balance. "Get the hell off my property!"

"Has your father ever met any of your boyfriends?" the reporter continued.

Benny decided to step in and do what Daniel had asked of him. He moved to stand in front of Jamie, his back to Tony, who was still trying to get the reporter off his driveway. "Hi, Jamie, I'm Benny. Daniel asked me to get you away from the media for your own good."

Jamie stared up at Benny. "The last thing Tony needs is trouble with the media. Bianchi Bytes has been in negotiations to buy another tech firm for months and any negative press could sink the deal. No way am I leaving him here to fight my battles for me."

Benny turned around to shield Jamie with his body as he tried to come up with a plan to get the reporter and camera operator off the Bianchi property. He eventually decided to start with the loudest of the two men and strode toward the reporter.

"Sorry, sir, but you've been told to vacate the premises." Without another word, Benny bent over and shoved his shoulder into the reporter's midsection before lifting him off the ground like a sack of potatoes. He easily carried the overweight reporter down the long driveway to the news van on the street while the man beat him with his microphone.

"Stay put," Benny growled once he'd set the man back on his feet. He turned and pointed to the cameraman, who had followed them, but still stood on the Bianchi estate. "You're next," he warned.

The camera operator had the good sense to hold up one arm in surrender. "I'm going." When he walked by Benny, he shook his head. "That was awesome. I've never seen anything like it."

Tony jogged down the drive to stand beside Benny. "Next time you step foot on my property, I'll call the cops."

"This story's not going to die down until you talk to us," the reporter yelled after Jamie, who was making his way through the gate. "The voters have a right to know the truth about where your father stands on your lifestyle!"

Benny had no idea what the man was talking about, but no one deserved to be ambushed like that. He crossed his arms over his bare chest. "I think you should go."

The reporter turned his microphone on Benny. "Who are you to Everett Whitmore III? Are you a love interest? Do you have anything you'd like to say to the people of Connecticut?"

Benny glanced at the microphone. "You have two seconds to get that out of my fucking face before I ram it down your throat."

"Is that a confirmation that you are indeed dating Everett Whitmore III?" the reporter pushed.

Benny took two steps forward, but Tony grabbed his arm.

"Don't," Tony warned. "He's on public property. If you touch him, he can file charges against you, and that's not the way you want to start your football career." He tugged Benny's forearm. "Come on. I've called my head of security. He'll be here any minute to make sure this asshole doesn't break the law again."

Benny hated backing down, but he understood Tony's point. "Okay." He eyed the reporter once more before turning to retrace his steps to the party. "Mind telling me what's going on?" he asked Tony.

"I would, but I think you should ask Jamie. From the impression I get, he doesn't have many friends here, so I'm sure he could use someone other than Daniel or Rocco to talk to." Tony opened the gate and waited for Benny to walk through before latching it behind him. "If you don't mind, I need to speak to Daniel about the security team that's about to invade our house."

"Sure." Benny left Tony and walked to the pool house. He felt uncomfortable about butting into Jamie's business, but from what he'd gathered, Jamie was dealing with some serious shit. Oblivious to the loud party going on around him, he knocked on the French door.

It took a moment, but the door eventually opened. Jamie's eyes were rimmed in red, a sure sign that he'd shed at least a few tears. "Hey." He stepped back and allowed Benny to enter. "Sorry about that."

"Nothing for you to apologize for. From the sound of it, your dad must be someone important," Benny said.

"You could say that." Jamie flopped down on a deep, pale blue sofa and gestured for Benny to do the same. "I've wanted to talk to you since I saw you last week at Clean Slate, but this definitely wasn't what I had in mind."

"Mind if I ask?" Benny prompted.

Jamie chuckled. "I take it you don't follow politics?"

Benny shook his head. "Sorry."

"Don't be. I hate politicians, and my dad is one. He's the senior senator from Connecticut, and one of those self-righteous bastards who believe homosexuals will lead the country into chaos if allowed the same rights as the straight majority. Ten days ago, I came out to him because I decided I was tired of living a lie." Jamie waved toward the door. "The reporter was here because the guy running against my father in the next election found out I'm gay and leaked a picture of me dancing in a bar to the press."

"Damn." Despite his dad's relationships embarrassing him on occasion, he was ultimately thankful he'd never had to go through what Jamie was suffering. "I can't imagine not having my dad's support. That has to be rough."

"It is," Jamie admitted. "What about your mom? Is she okay with it, too?"

"Mom died when I was young." Benny had no idea why he was opening up to Jamie, but he felt comfortable with him. "Dad's a cop, and he moved us to Cattle Valley after she died." He glanced at Jamie. "Are you familiar with Cattle Valley?"

"Sure. I doubt there's many gay men in the United States that haven't heard about it."

"Yeah, well, what I didn't know when we moved there was that my dad is gay. He's now in a relationship with two men, Ethan and Pete. They're good guys. Pete's a deputy like Dad, and Ethan works in the mayor's office."

"I'm sorry to hear about your mom," Jamie said. "I'm closest to my mother, but she refuses to stand up to my father, so we didn't part on good terms either."

The two of them sat in silence for several moments. "Should we rejoin the party?" Benny finally asked. "I'm starving."

When Benny rubbed his stomach, he was delighted to see the raw desire in Jamie's gaze as he followed the path of Benny's hand with his eyes. *Interesting.* He got to his feet and stretched his arms over his head, giving Jamie the full show. *Hell.* His heart may still belong to Chase, but it had been too long since he'd held someone. The way he saw it, if Chase could let another man fuck him every night, why couldn't Benny do the same thing with someone else — at least until Chase came to his senses? He stared down at the sexy-as-fuck man with hair begging to be wrapped around his hand. Jamie was leaner than Chase, which would also be a new experience. *Yeah.* What he needed was more experience so he could blow Chase's mind once they were back together. "Ready?"

Lips slightly parted, Jamie nodded.

Benny led the way out of the pool house. It felt good to be wanted.

* * * *

"Are you sure you don't want something to eat?" Benny asked, standing above Jamie on the pool deck.

From his position in the water, Jamie shook his head. "I'm not hungry." Truth was, his cock was as hard as steel and there was no way he was going to get out of the water in his present condition.

"Okay. Let me grab a couple of burgers, and I can dangle my feet in the pool while I eat."

Jamie sighed as he watched Benny walk in the direction of the food table. The sight of Benny's muscular back and ass did absolutely nothing to calm his raging hard-on.

Stretched out on a foam float, Rocco drifted by Jamie. "You doing okay?"

Jamie wasn't sure if his new friend was referring to the episode earlier with the reporter or the very real possibility that something could happen with Benny. The answer to both was simple. "Yeah."

Rocco glanced toward the buffet table. "He's really big."

"Yep, I kinda noticed," Jamie agreed.

"And he thinks he's still in love with his high school boyfriend. Be careful, man. Right now he's still young, dumb and full of cum."

Jamie rolled his eyes at the old saying. "Maybe, but I'm not looking for a life partner, just someone to pass the time with while I'm here."

"It won't be enough," Rocco warned. "Trust me."

Rocco floated away moments before Benny returned with a plate loaded with food. He eased his large frame down to the pool's edge, sank his calves into the clear water and spread his legs.

"I brought you a drink," Benny said, placing a bottle of water between his legs.

Jamie met Benny's gaze, wondering at the obvious game. "That for me?"

Benny took a bite of one of his hamburgers. "If you want it."

A shiver rose up Jamie's spine. Benny's voice was as deep as he was big and it seemed to grow even deeper when he was aroused. One look at the half-hard cock pressed against the thin fabric of Benny's swimsuit proved to Jamie that the offensive lineman was definitely ready to play.

Jamie moved to insinuate himself between Benny's muscular thighs. The bottle was snug against Benny's erection, leaving Jamie a provocative invitation.

Benny lifted his plate higher to give Jamie headroom. Unfortunately, it also cut off Jamie's view of Benny's handsome face. Oh well, Jamie would have to be satisfied with Benny's lower half for the moment. He rested his forearms on Benny's legs as he reached for the bottle. When the back of his hand pressed against the impossibly large bulge, Jamie had to stifle a groan. He wrapped his hand around the plastic to hold it in place as he unscrewed the cap with his other hand.

"Too bad you didn't grab a straw. I could've buried my head in your lap and sucked it that way." Jamie didn't even blush at the lewd statement. He'd never been a tease because he'd never had time to waste on subtleties. However, when he heard Benny's grunt of approval and saw the tightening of Benny's abdominal muscles, Jamie decided foreplay could be a lot of fun.

"Careful," Benny rumbled. He lowered his plate to the smooth natural stone that made up the pool deck. "You're giving me all sorts of ideas."

Jamie noticed the amount of food Benny had consumed in the short amount of time they'd been talking and decided Benny had had enough for the moment. "Why don't you slide into the water, and I'll give you a few more?"

Benny narrowed his eyes before scanning the area. The party was still in full swing, but Benny evidently didn't care because a second later, he was in the pool with his hands on Jamie's hips.

Jamie grinned. Benny was so tall the water barely covered his erection. "Maybe we should swim to the deeper end?"

"What'll your friends think?" Benny asked.

Jamie spotted Daniel sitting on Tony's lap, talking to Rocco and Joe. "They're not even paying attention to us." As soon as the words left Jamie's lips, Daniel winked at him. He winked back.

Benny moved his hips from side to side, rubbing his cock against Jamie's stomach.

"I'm two seconds away from wrapping my legs around your waist so that log you have in your trunks'll rub against my dick," Jamie told Benny. "We can do that here or in the deep end. Your choice."

When Benny didn't move fast enough, Jamie placed his hands on Benny's shoulders and hoisted himself up. Benny steadied Jamie by putting his hands on Jamie's ass. With a chuckle, Benny started walking. "How does Tony feel about cum in his pool?"

Jamie licked a path up Benny's thick neck. "I don't know. You want to ask him?"

"Fuck," Benny groaned in Jamie's ear as he began to knead Jamie's butt. "You're killin' me."

The fact that Benny was only eighteen meant he could probably go all night, but it also meant he probably didn't have the control of someone older. Jamie decided it would be best to cool things a bit before he really did make Benny come. He pointed to a niche in the natural stones that lined the water. Benny was too big to fit into the space, but Jamie wasn't. "There."

Benny backed Jamie into the narrow recess. "You need to know this is purely sexual because I'm planning to get back with my boyfriend."

Jamie didn't tell Benny that he knew about Chase or that he was well aware Chase was in a committed relationship with Mac. "Sex is good." He pushed his hand under the waistband of Benny's trunks. *Holy fucking shit!* "And if it's great, maybe you'll use me for as long as it takes to get your man back," he added after his first touch of Benny's impressive dick.

Benny groaned when Jamie took hold of his erection. "We can probably work something out," he whispered against Jamie's lips.

Jamie teased Benny's mouth with the tip of his tongue for several heartbeats before delving inside for a proper taste. He barely managed to get what he wanted before Benny took over the kiss. If Jamie was the kind of man who cared about asserting his dominance, Benny's action would have angered him, but Jamie was a go-with-the-flow type of guy. He happily gave control to Benny because he was interested to see what Benny would do with it.

Benny didn't disappoint when he kissed Jamie with a mastery that belied his years.

Jamie melted in Benny's strong embrace as the erotic kiss continued. What had Chase been thinking to give up a man like Benny? *Christ.* Jamie could happily spend the next hundred years being dominated by the man currently fucking his mouth with his tongue.

Benny pulled out of the kiss, and Jamie actually whimpered at the loss. "What?" Jamie asked.

"Invite me into the pool house," Benny ordered.

* * * *

In front of Locky, Becket and about fifteen other guys from the dorm, Benny carried Jamie up the steps, out of the water and to the house. He hadn't seen a bedroom earlier, but the structure appeared large enough to have one. "Bed," he growled upon entering Jamie's private space.

"Through the door on the right," Jamie said between sucking bites to Benny's neck.

Benny had no doubt everyone at the party knew exactly what he and Jamie were about to do, and even if word got back to Chase, he found he didn't care at the moment. The only thing on his mind was stripping Jamie and burying his cock deep. He pushed open the door Jamie had indicated and groaned when he spotted the California King with rumpled sheets. It had been over a week since he'd been blessed with a good night's sleep.

Benny released his hold on Jamie before pushing his wet swim trunks down. "You have condoms?"

Jamie's hazel eyes rounded as he stared down at Benny's dark-skinned shaft. "Yeah, but I don't know if they'll fit."

"They'll fit for now. Next time I come over, I'll bring my own." Benny waited for Jamie to strip out of his clothes and retrieve a box of condoms and bottle of lube before he tossed the smaller man onto the bed. Towering over Jamie, Benny took a moment to notice the differences between Chase's body and Jamie's. He found himself trailing his finger down the dark brown line of hair below Jamie's bellybutton to the short patch of equally dark pubic hair that surrounded a nice cock. The hair on Chase's head was light blond but his pubic hair had a reddish tint to it. Oddly, Benny thought perhaps he preferred the darker hair against Jamie's sun-bronzed skin. "So sexy," he mumbled.

Jamie spread his legs, giving Benny a better view. "You're one to talk. I feel like I'm getting ready to be fucked by a fantasy version of a Marvel comic book hero."

One thing was for sure, Benny had needed the boost of confidence Jamie gave him. After what had happened with Chase, he'd felt inadequate. So much so that he hadn't been interested in sex until he'd set eyes on Jamie at Clean Slate. He still wasn't sure what it was about Jamie that had captured his attention that night, but he definitely remembered the feelings of guilt that had swamped him before he'd returned his gaze to Chase. At the moment, however, he didn't feel an ounce of guilt over what he was about to do to the man sprawled out on the bed.

Benny wrapped his hand around his erection and gave the shaft several strokes as he tried to decide where he wanted to start.

Legs still spread wide, Jamie bent his knees and planted his feet on the mattress. "Hand me the lube?"

Benny retrieved the bottle from the table and tossed it to Jamie. He wasn't sure what Jamie was about to do, but he had a feeling he was going to like it a lot.

Jamie dripped lube onto his fingers before reaching between his legs.

Benny sucked in a breath as he watched one long, slim finger disappear into Jamie's hole. "Fuck." He couldn't remember Chase ever being so bold in front of him. He reached for a condom and tore open the package with his teeth. "You're gonna have to fit a lot more than that in there before I can take you."

Jamie chuckled. "Yeah, got that," he replied before adding another finger. He used his free hand to cup and knead his balls as he continued to plunge long digits in and out of his hole. "It's been a few months for me, so go easy."

"Don't worry, babe. It's been longer than that for me," Benny confessed.

"How long?"

"Since Christmas." The last time Benny had been with Chase, he'd known something was off between them. It hadn't been that he'd found Chase any less sexy, but the heat between them had cooled considerably after Chase had left for college. Benny had chalked it up to not seeing each other often enough and had begged Chase on more than one occasion to let him visit the school he'd soon attend. Each time Benny had asked though, Chase had come up with an excuse — usually work related.

Jamie had worked his way up to three fingers by the time Benny's patience had run out. "That's enough," Benny growled. He put one knee on the bed before lowering himself on top of Jamie. "How do you want it?" he whispered against Jamie's lips.

"Any way I can get it," Jamie replied as he wrapped his legs around Benny's waist.

Benny reached between them and fit the head of his sheathed cock to Jamie's stretched opening. He gritted his teeth as he fought the urge to ram inside and come. *Fuck.* He probably should've jacked off while he watched Jamie finger himself. "Distract me," he urged.

"Huh?"

Benny took a deep breath. "I'm too close, so distract me. Tell me what your major is?"

"Okay, umm, until a week ago, I was on track to get a degree in political science, but I've decided to thumb my nose at what my father wants me to do with my life and graduate with a ceramics degree," Jamie explained as he hitched his legs higher around Benny's torso.

"Ceramics degree? Is that a real thing?" Benny asked. He eased his length in further.

"Yeah, it's a real thing." Jamie dug his short nails into the back of Benny's shoulders. "What about you?"

"Haven't decided. I figure I'll either end up a coach, or a cop like my dad. That is, of course, if I don't get drafted by a pro team." Benny prayed the next four years would see an increase in out-and-proud players because he wouldn't hide who he was for anyone or anything.

"It's working." Benny rocked his hips, giving Jamie a few more inches. "You ever had a serious boyfriend?"

Jamie shook his head. "I've never denied my sexuality, but I've had to be discreet up until now. Most guys I've met since starting school don't know the meaning of the word, so I've always just hooked-up with random guys for a night or two."

"This'll be the first time I've had sex without being in love," Benny admitted. He needed to make sure Jamie understood theirs wasn't a love connection. The reminder also served to cool his ardor enough to fully penetrate Jamie without coming.

"You're lucky."

"I thought I was." Benny felt his cock begin to soften. "Okay, no more talk." He lowered his head and thrust his tongue into Jamie's mouth in an attempt to refuel his erection. The kiss worked and soon Jamie was writhing under him.

"Move," Jamie croaked.

Benny used his upper body strength to push up off Jamie until he was seated on his heels. The new position allowed him to watch as his cock stroked in and out of Jamie's tight ass. A cross between a moan and a grunt escaped Jamie each time Benny thrust his hips. "You like that?"

Jamie opened his eyes and stared up at Benny. "Now I know you're a damn superhero."

"Which one?" Benny wrapped his hand around Jamie's dick and started to pump.

"I don't know. Which one has the biggest muscles and cock?" Jamie asked.

"The Hulk?" Benny suggested, picking up speed.

"You're too handsome to be the Hulk. Maybe Thor," Jamie offered.

"I'm too black to be Thor." Benny stopped thinking about superheroes when Jamie's body jerked and tightened around him.

"Oh fuck!" Jamie shouted as he coated Benny's hand in warm cum.

Free to be selfish, Benny began pumping into Jamie with his own release in mind. It only took three cock-burying thrusts to tip him over the edge. He came with a growl and a silent plea to make it last longer the next time.

Once Benny's breathing calmed, he withdrew from Jamie and eased off the condom. "Trash can?"

"Over by the desk." Jamie threw his forearm over his eyes. "Goliath. Definitely Goliath."

"Is he black?" Benny asked as he tied off the rubber. He grabbed the trash can before relocating it beside the bed.

"Don't you know your superheroes?" Jamie asked.

"Not really. Although I know the Ambiguously Gay Duo from Saturday Night Live." Benny crawled into bed beside Jamie and threw the cover over his chilled skin.

Laughing, Jamie snuggled close and wrapped an arm around Benny's waist. "I'd forgotten about those cartoons. Ace and Gary. Classic!" He trailed his fingertips up and down Benny's chest. "Are you staying?"

"Are you asking?" The last thing Benny wanted was to leave the big bed or the man in it.

"Absolutely." Jamie sucked Benny's nipple into his mouth before releasing it with a popping sound.

"Then yeah, I'd love to stay." Benny settled his hand on the cheek of Jamie's ass. "How long do you think the party will last?"

"I don't care because the only one I want to party with is you." Jamie rolled on top of Benny. "I hope I have enough condoms to last the night."

Benny glanced at the box of twelve. They'd already used one and he could see them using several more before they went to sleep for the night. "We've got plenty for tonight, but we'll have to go easy in the morning until I can get to my stash back at the dorm."

Jamie chuckled and buried his face against Benny's neck. "Where the hell have you been all my life?"

It was obvious by the way Jamie had said it that he had meant it as a joke, but Benny's mind immediately went to Chase. He wrapped his arms around Jamie while he tried like hell to push thoughts of Chase from his mind. "I think there's a Mariners game on. Care if I watch a while?"

Jamie lifted his head and looked down at Benny. "You're a Seattle fan?

"Yeah. What's wrong with that?" Benny asked.

Jamie reached to the bedside table and retrieved the remote. "Nothing if you want to watch a bunch of girls play, but if you'd rather watch real baseball, you should find a Red Sox game."

Benny turned the television on. "Good thing I'm not done fucking you because those're fightin' words."

"Yeah. Yeah." Jamie moved enough to see the game and settled in.

Chapter Four

"Are any of these yours?" Benny asked as he studied the shelves of bowls, vases and platters.

"No, those are Daniel's. He likes to make practical items someone can actually use on a daily basis if they want." Jamie gestured to the various statues on the top shelf. "He's probably best known for his sculptures, though."

Benny had never been into art, but he was interested in Jamie's work. Not because he thought he'd gain a new appreciation for bowls or vases but because for some reason, he found himself fascinated by Jamie. "So, is there something in here of yours?"

Jamie smiled and crooked his finger. "I'm not as fast as Rocco or Daniel, but I get off on knowing each piece I create is unique." He led Benny to the far corner of the large studio and turned his back as he squatted down to take something off the bottom shelf.

"This is my latest." Jamie faced Benny while clutching the most beautiful vase Benny had ever set eyes on.

When Jamie held it out, Benny crossed his arms and shook his head. "No, I'm not touching that."

Jamie's expression fell. "You don't like it?"

Benny tore his gaze away from the vase. "No. I love it. I've never seen anything like it." He uncrossed his arms and held up his hands. "I don't do well with delicate things, though, and I'd never forgive myself if I broke it."

"It would mean a lot to me if you'd keep it."

Taking a deep breath, Benny took the gift Jamie had so thoughtfully given. He traced the intricate design. "How do you do it?"

"It's called cutwork. After I make the vase, I carve the design before I glaze and fire it. Sometimes, I choose to cut all the way through the clay, like this one." He retrieved another vase, this one was covered in realistic wildflowers. "Other times, I carve out just enough clay to create these relief designs."

Benny shook his head. "I had no idea. I mean, I've seen fancy stuff like this in stores, but I guess I never thought about someone actually making them." He stared down at the work of art in his hands. "Can I watch you do one?"

"Sure." Jamie set the wildflower vase back on the shelf before slipping a denim apron over his head. "Go ahead and grab Rocco's stool. I doubt he'll be in today anyway."

For the next hour, Benny sat mesmerized as he watched Jamie work. He couldn't imagine Jamie sitting in political science classes when he had the talent to create such beauty. When he noticed the time, he groaned. "Shit. I've gotta go."

Jamie looked up from the urn he'd been working on. "Will you be over tonight?"

"Yeah." Benny gave Jamie a deep kiss. He hated leaving, but he couldn't be late for practice.

* * * *

Benny bounded down the hall toward his room. He'd spent yet another afternoon watching Jamie work. His addiction to Jamie had gotten so bad that Daniel had actually bought Benny a comfortable chair for Jamie's corner of the studio. He threw open the door and came to an abrupt halt.

Ira Rhinehart, his new roommate, was sitting on Benny's bed, completely naked with a video game controller in his hands, playing a game on Benny's fucking TV. Before Benny could explode, Twitch jumped a mile in the air before falling off the end of the mattress.

Yeah, there was a reason Benny had nicknamed the guy Twitch. "What the fuck're you doing?"

"Sorry, man." Twitch crawled on his hands and knees back to his side of the room. "You're never here, so I didn't think you'd mind."

"Didn't think I'd mind? You're sitting naked on my fucking bed!" Benny grabbed his workout bag. "I don't care if you play games, but stay off my fucking bed!" It didn't matter that he hadn't slept in his bed for nearly three weeks, it was still his. He stuffed a set of clean clothes into the duffle. "And put some goddamn clothes on. Fuck!"

Benny left the room without another word. He stormed down the stairs and went straight to Locky's office. "You got a second?"

"Sure, come in," Locky greeted him through the open door. "What's up?"

"Twitch. Can you have a talk with him and tell him he needs to put on some damn clothes? I'm sick of walking into my room to find a naked, pale, one hundred pound nerd lounging around."

Locky sighed and ran his fingers through his hair. "I'm sorry. Ira's having a hard time adjusting. He grew up in a nudist colony and claims clothes stifle his inner light."

"That's not true." Benny thought Locky was messing with him.

"Actually, it is. His first evening here, he came down to dinner without clothes. Believe me, the only one not scandalized was Charlie."

Benny shook his head. He knew Charlie hadn't been shocked because the guy was blind so couldn't have seen Twitch.

Locky leaned back in his chair. "We're hoping to put him in a private room the second one becomes available, so just be patient."

"Right." Benny wanted to argue that he shouldn't have to live with a nudist, but he was definitely going to be late for practice. "Until that happens, I'll do my best to stay elsewhere."

"That shouldn't be hard since you and Jamie seem attached at the hip lately."

For some reason, Benny felt the need to explain why he was spending so much time with Jamie. "Besides the fact that I actually fit in Jamie's bed, he's going through some shit right now. Between the reporters and the non-stop calls from his folks, he needs a friend."

Locky nodded several times before turning it into a shake of his head. "I don't know how he's going to start classes on Monday without the campus turning into a three-ring circus."

"Daniel's already worked that out with administration. Until the reporters move on to another story, Jamie's being allowed independent study for his art classes. It helps a lot that Tony built a studio at the house, so Jamie doesn't even have to leave the property." Benny glanced at the clock. "Sorry. I need to get to practice before Bear eats me."

Chuckling, Locky waved him off. "Go. I'll do what I can to get your room situation sorted."

"Thanks." Instead of running across campus, Benny jumped into his car since he'd promised Jamie he'd be over later anyway. On the way to the field, he wondered if Chase would talk to him after practice. It didn't make sense to him. On the field, he and Chase worked well together, so much so it felt like they were reliving their high school glory days when they'd taken Cattle Valley to the Wyoming State Championship and had won two years straight. Off the field, Chase barely looked at him, and had yet to speak with him like he'd promised.

Benny groaned when he spotted the shiny Harley parked in front of the athletic building. He had no doubt to whom the bike belonged. Rage boiled up in Benny. It was bad enough that he had to think about Chase fucking another guy. The last thing he needed was to actually see the two of them together.

The locker room was empty when Benny entered. No surprise since practice had officially started ten minutes earlier, and players were required to be on the field and dressed before the coaches arrived.

It took Benny another five minutes to get his gear on—a record for him. He jogged out to the field, prepared for the ass-chewing he would receive. He just prayed Bear didn't bench him over the infraction.

"Nice of you to show up today, Benny!" Bear yelled. He pointed to the stadium seats. "Stairs. Now!"

Benny groaned. He hated running the fucking stairs. Usually Bear allowed the offense to run them in the morning, before the heat of the day, but evidently Bear wanted to see Benny puke. So be it. He knew there was no way he'd get out of it. He hoped it would be his only punishment, but he doubted it.

Benny spotted a tattooed older man leaning against the fence and knew in his gut it was Mac. Intent on speaking to Chase's new sex partner, Benny headed toward him.

"What part of stairs do you not understand, Benny!" Bear shouted over the usual noise of practice.

Since Benny's first day on the field, Bear had used Steamroller as a nickname for him. The fact that his coach was suddenly referring to him as Benny said a lot about Bear's mood, so Benny decided not to push it. He headed for the steps and started what would become the worst torture he'd ever endured.

After an hour of running up and down the grandstand, the cramping began. He stopped at the bottom and bent over at the waist in an attempt to alleviate the pain and catch his breath.

"Get going!" Bear screamed with not an ounce of mercy in his tone.

When Benny glanced at his coach, he was shocked to see Chase arguing with Bear. It was then that he noticed half the team were watching Benny with pity in their eyes. *Screw that.* No way would he let Bear get the best of him.

With a renewed sense of purpose, Benny pushed the pain aside and started back up the steps. Fifteen minutes later, his legs collapsed under him halfway up the rise. His mouth filled with spit and he braced himself for the inevitable. It didn't take long before he threw up the entire contents of his stomach.

"Are you okay?" Chase asked, bounding up the steps behind Benny.

"Chase!" Bear yelled. "Hit the showers!"

Benny closed his eyes and rested his forehead on the step next to the vomit he'd expelled.

"Here." Chase knelt down beside Benny and handed him a bottle of water. "Small sips," he reminded Benny.

Instead of making Benny feel better, Chase's concern pissed him off. "Go," Benny managed to say between pants.

"I'm not going anywhere. This is bullshit, and Bear knows it." Chase rested his palm on Benny's back. "Come on. I'll help you down the steps."

"You've ignored me since day one. What makes you think I'll accept your attention now?" Benny grimaced as another round of wracking pain seized his stomach.

"Chase," Bear growled from behind them. "Get your fucking ass back on that field before you suffer the same fate as your friend."

Chase stared up at Bear. "Coach, he's bad. Believe me, I know Benny like no one else here, and I can tell you, this is bad."

Despite his agony, warmth filled Benny at Chase's words.

"Maybe so, but that's my problem. Not yours. Go!" Bear huffed.

Chase squeezed Benny's shoulder. "Tomorrow. I promise we can talk after practice."

"If I live that long," Benny muttered.

After Chase had retreated, Bear took a seat on one of the chairs a row up from where Benny still knelt on the cement. "I know what's going on in that big head of yours, and the best thing you can do for yourself is to forget it."

Benny peered up at his coach. The profound respect he'd always felt for Bear left him in an instant. "You don't know what the hell you're talking about."

"Yeah?" Bear leaned down, putting himself closer to Benny. "That boy's in love with someone else, and you refuse to accept that your time with him is over. You're so damn consumed with getting him back that you can't see the forest for the trees. Mac and Chase are the real deal, and the sooner you realize that, the sooner you can get on with your life."

Benny heaved and the water he'd just drank came right back up. "Are you telling me this whole stairs exercise has been about my feelings for Chase?"

"Hell no. You earned this lesson, boy. No one, and I mean no one, gets away with coming to practice late without suffering the stairs. Rule one. I told you that the first day." Bear got to his feet. "Lay here as long as you need to. Then hit the locker room. You're done for the day."

* * * *

Jamie carried his plate to the sink. It had been the first night he'd had dinner in the main house since Tony had returned from South America. He rinsed his plate before loading it into the dishwasher.

"Thanks for cooking," Daniel said, coming into the kitchen.

"It was the least I could do." Jamie took the plates from Daniel before repeating the procedure. "Still no word from BK House. I'm starting to wonder if I should just try to get a room in the regular dorms."

Daniel leaned his hip against the counter. "I talked it over with Tony, and we'd like you to stay for as long as you want. You've got enough going on without worrying about a place to live. Besides, you're, like, the perfect tenant."

Jamie had tried his best to stay out of Tony and Daniel's way when they were together. He even made a point to keep the blinds closed on the windows that looked out to the pool because he knew the pair enjoyed swimming in the nude before going to bed. "At least let me pay you something while I'm here."

"Did you suddenly win the lottery?" Daniel asked.

"I wish." Jamie shook his head. "I've got a little money that my father can't get his hands on."

"Yeah, and you'll need every penny until you start selling your work," Daniel reminded him before letting out a long sigh. "Seriously, Tony doesn't need your money, and he really does like that I'm not alone when he has to travel."

Jamie bit his lip. Living in the pool house really was the perfect place for him. Not only did he have more privacy than he'd get in the dorm, but the studio was only steps away, and Tony's guards kept the reporters at bay. "Okay, but you have to promise that you'll tell me if you guys change your minds. I consider you both friends and, believe me, I can use all of those I can get right now."

"Great. It's settled," Daniel said just as the house phone started to ring. His eyes narrowed. "No one ever calls the house."

"Probably the press." Jamie picked up the phone, ready to tear the reporter a new asshole for bothering Daniel and Tony. "What?"

"Umm, is this Professor Willis' house?"

"Who wants to know?" Jamie asked.

"This is Chase Hughes. I need to get a message to Jamie Whitmore."

Christ. Why was Benny's ex calling? "This is Jamie," he replied. "What do you want?"

"Oh, hey." Chase paused. "I thought you should know that Coach Tucker made Benny run stairs today to punish him for being late to practice. When I left the field, Benny was still sitting on the steps in the grandstand. I'll be honest, I'm worried about him. Coach said Benny would be fine, but I'm not convinced."

"Sorry, I don't know what running steps means." Jamie glanced at Daniel when he heard Daniel groan. He could tell by the expression on Daniel's face that it wasn't good.

"If you break a rule, you have to run up and down the stadium steps until the coach believes you've learned your lesson. For Benny, that lesson lasted almost an hour and a half. As far as I know, that's the longest anyone's lasted without collapsing," Chase explained. "Anyway, I'm worried about him, but I don't want to give him false hope. You can trust me when I say that part of my life is over."

Jamie exhaled. "Can I ask you a question?"

"Sure."

"How'd you know to call me?" Jamie asked.

"Word gets around," Chase replied. "I know Benny, and if he's spent every night at your place, he must really like you."

"It's just sex for Benny," Jamie told Chase. It was the same mantra he had to repeat to himself daily.

"No it isn't. He might have told you that, and he may even believe it, but Benny isn't made that way. If you truly like him, hang in there."

"Why're you telling me all this?" Jamie didn't understand why he was having such a personal conversation with Benny's ex.

"Because I figured something out when I met Mac. Benny and I were friends more than anything else. Sure, we had sex once in a while, but we were more passionate talking about football or fishing than we were in each other's arms. And, I guess, I miss my friend, but I know I can't get that back until he realizes what we really meant to each other."

"I see." Jamie didn't know what else to say. "You really think he's still at the stadium?"

"I can't be positive, but he was still sitting there when the rest of the team finished for the day."

"Okay, I'll check on him. Thanks for letting me know." Jamie hung up. "Do you think you can get me outta here without the press following us?"

Daniel's face lit with an evil grin. "Absolutely."

* * * *

Jamie wasn't surprised to find several vehicles, including Benny's, still parked in front of the athletic building when he arrived.

"That's Bear's truck," Daniel pointed out. "I didn't think Bear would go home and leave one of his players still on the field."

"You don't have to wait. I'll drive Benny's car back to the house," Jamie said, sliding out of Tony's big black Escalade. "Thanks for the ride."

"No problem. I'll talk to you tomorrow," Daniel replied, putting the SUV into gear.

"Yeah." Jamie threw up a hand before turning toward the building. He didn't bother knocking, instead he walked straight in and followed the signs to the coaches' offices.

"Hello?" Jamie stopped outside a room with four men huddled around a television. "Coach Tucker?"

A huge black man, nearly as big as Benny, stood. "I'm Bear."

"I came to take Benny home. Can you tell me where I'll find him?"

Bear stepped out of the room before closing the door behind him. He gestured for Jamie to follow as he headed down the hall. "I made him come in about thirty minutes ago." He stopped outside the locker room. "From the sound of it, he's still in the shower. Do me a favor and get him to stop wasting water."

Intimidated by the aptly named man, Jamie nodded.

"You're Jamie, right?" Bear asked.

"Yeah."

Bear nodded once. "See that he's not late to practice again, will ya?"

"Sure, but can you explain why his punishment was so severe just for being late?" Jamie couldn't believe he'd had the guts to ask, but he wanted to know what kind of man Benny was playing under.

"You've never played football, have you?"

Jamie looked down at his lean body. "What was your first clue?"

Bear grinned. "Trust in your fellow teammates is the most important part of football. The quarterback counts on the protection his offensive line give him. If he doesn't have trust, he can't play to the best of his ability, and if he doesn't do that, you don't win games. I know the shit going on between Benny and Chase, and that shit's landed at my feet because the two of them don't trust each other anymore. When Benny showed up late, it wasn't simply a matter of time on the clock. We'd already run a few drills and Chase didn't have Benny there to protect him from the defensive tackles. I needed to punish Benny in a way that he'll probably never forget. Believe me, it wasn't fun for me, but I knew it was necessary to get through to him. Not only did I make Benny run stairs, but I made Chase sit out of practice because I also need Chase to understand that without Benny there, he's not going to play. Hopefully it worked and the two of them will stop the bullshit."

Jamie didn't understand Bear's reasoning, but he wasn't a coach, so he had to assume Bear had Benny's best interests at heart. "Okay."

"We're getting ready to head out. I'll lock the door. Just make sure you pull it closed when you leave."

"Yes, sir," Jamie replied.

"He'll probably need potassium, so get him fed and rub him down when he gets home," Bear instructed before disappearing down the hall.

Jamie entered the locker room and walked in the direction of the showers. He wasn't sure if Benny would welcome his intrusion into the situation, so he decided to fall back on the one thing they had in common. He quickly undressed and stacked his folded clothes onto one of the benches.

When Jamie rounded the corner, he saw Benny sitting with his back against the wall, head in his hands while the water sprayed down on him. Jamie tested the water and found it to be freezing cold. He turned off the shower before sliding down the wall next to Benny.

"What're you doing here?" Benny asked.

Jamie leaned his head against Benny's muscular arm. If he told Benny the truth, he would probably make the situation between Benny and Chase worse, so he decided to lie. "I was incredibly horny, and I couldn't wait for you to come over, so I thought I'd jump you in the shower."

Benny lifted his arm, giving Jamie room to scoot closer. "You hear what Coach did to me?"

"Yeah," Jamie confessed. "He told me to take you home, feed you and rub you down. I didn't tell him that had become our normal routine anyway."

Benny wrapped his arm around Jamie a little tighter. "It was embarrassing. Mac was at practice with Chase. The first time Mac sees me, and I'm puking my guts out after running a few steps."

"From what I heard, you ran more than a few," Jamie corrected.

"Who told you?"

Jamie turned his head and kissed Benny's chest. He liked the quiet moment between them and didn't want to bring Chase into it. "Chase called Daniel, and I answered the phone, thinking it was a reporter."

"Chase?" Benny sat up a little straighter.

Jamie nodded. "He said he misses his friend, but he can't go there with you because you'd take it the wrong way."

"What the fuck does that mean? You can't just be friends with someone you're still in love with."

"I swear, you say fuck more than anyone I've ever met," Jamie barked. He knew it wasn't the word that had pissed him off—it was Benny's continued obsession with Chase.

Benny laughed. "Fuck's a great word. It's versatile."

Jamie shrugged out of Benny's hold. "Come on. I see a few dozen bananas in your future," he said as he got to his feet.

Benny grabbed Jamie's hand and pulled him into his lap. "Not yet." He rested his hands on Jamie's butt. "Did you bring condoms with you?"

Jamie reared back. "Seriously? Despite what I said earlier, I came here because I was worried about you."

"Don't be. I told you from the beginning that I only needed you for sex until Chase pulled his head out of his ass."

Hurt by the callous comment, Jamie pushed his way out of Benny's lap. "You're a real sonofabitch, you know that?" He got to his feet and stared down at Benny. "The sex has been fantastic, but I thought you enjoyed my company outside of bed, too. I was a fool for believing I could ever mean more to you than a stand-in hole."

"Calm down," Benny admonished.

"No. To use your favorite word, fuck you!" Jamie ran out of the shower.

"Jamie. Come back," Benny called.

Jamie pulled on his clothes without bothering to dry himself first and was out of the door within three minutes. It wasn't until he reached the parking lot that he remembered he didn't have his car or his phone. He reached to his back pocket and felt around. *Christ.* He hadn't even bothered to grab his wallet.

He could probably go to BK House and get a ride home, but the last thing he wanted was to run into Benny. Although walking wasn't really his gig, he decided to just hoof it the three miles home.

Chapter Five

By the time Benny made it to the dorm, he was in a foul mood. Instead of dealing with the naked idiot upstairs, he decided to park himself on the sofa in the rec room and watch some television.

Unfortunately, the longer he sat there, the guiltier he felt for the way things had gone down between him and Jamie. The only reason he'd initiated sex in the shower was to push thoughts of Chase from his mind. Well, that and being unable to stop thinking about Jamie's body no matter how many times they had sex. There was something about Jamie that worked like a drug on Benny, and for the life of him, he couldn't figure out what it was.

He pulled out his phone and texted Chase. It was something he hadn't done in a very long time, but he needed to make something very clear to Chase.

Hey, do me a favor and don't call Jamie again unless you want me to call Mac and tell him what I really think of him. B

Benny sent the message and waited for a response. After several minutes, his phone dinged.

Sorry. I was trying to help. Is he mad?

Benny refused to lie, but Chase needed to know what he'd done wasn't cool.

Not about the call, but it caused problems between us.

Benny hit send without bothering to sign the text. There had been a time when he'd ended all his texts to Chase with either Xs and Os or a declaration of love, but he doubted anything of that nature would be welcome at the moment.

That's too bad. Sorry. He seemed nice on the phone. I think he's really into you. I just want you to find happiness.

Benny scowled at the phone. Was Chase kidding?

I found happiness once, and I'm doing everything I can to get my happiness back, but you refuse to speak to me outside of practice.

By the end of the sentence, Benny found himself pounding on the screen.

Benny jumped when his phone rang. His heart squeezed when he saw Chase's name on the display. "Hey," he answered.

"It's time we talked. Meet me at Jerry's Sandwich Shoppe in an hour," Chase said, instead of a greeting. "You know where that is?"

"At the south end of campus?" Benny asked. He'd spent so much time with Jamie since he'd been in town, he hadn't done as much exploring as he probably should have. He would've liked to go out to eat or to the movies with Jamie, but it wasn't possible with the press still hanging around.

"Yeah, right across the street from the library," Chase confirmed.

"I'll be there." Benny ended the call. He was on his way to change into something nicer to wear when his phone rang again. The display said Daniel was calling. "Hello?" he answered.

"Hey, Benny, it's Daniel. Is Jamie with you?"

Benny squeezed his eyes shut. He hated to tell Daniel what a prick he'd been to Jamie—especially after Jamie had come to the locker room to cheer him up. "No. He, uhhh…" *Fuck.* "We had a fight, and he left."

"Left? How? He didn't take his car. I dropped him off."

"Then how'd he get home?" Benny asked.

"That's why I'm calling. He's not home, and his father's here," Daniel explained.

Despite being so sore he could barely move, Benny turned and headed to the front door. "I'll jump in my car and start looking. If he had it in his head to walk home, I should be able to find him."

"What should I tell his father? He's sitting out by the pool right now because Tony won't let him into our house." Daniel chuckled. "Tony's not fond of Republicans."

"You don't have to tell him anything. Let the bastard sit there. Maybe we'll all get lucky, and he'll give up and leave." Benny eased down the front steps.

Daniel's chuckle turned into a laugh. "Yeah, we can hope."

"I'm getting into my car now. I'll find Jamie and bring him home." Benny winced as he folded his sore body into the car. He was thankful he had the weekend to recuperate before he was expected back on the field. Bear was right about one thing—never again would Benny be late for practice.

"Call me, and, by the way, just because I haven't given you shit about whatever you did or said to make Jamie storm out on you, doesn't mean I'll forget about it."

Benny drove out of the parking lot. "Right. Later." He wouldn't blame Daniel for kicking him off his property once he'd found Jamie. Hell, Jamie had been dumped on enough lately. Between the reporters and his own family, the last thing Jamie needed was Benny dumping on him, too.

Benny cruised by the athletic department before heading in the direction of Tony's estate. He didn't know if Tony considered it an estate, but in Benny's mind a piece of property with a mansion, pool, pool house and pottery studio was considered a fucking estate. Only a sliver of the orange glow of the sun could be seen over the horizon, making the search for Jamie that much harder.

"Come on. Where are you?" he muttered to himself as he scanned the sidewalks for any sight of his sexy potter.

Benny had nearly reached Tony's place when his phone rang. He grabbed the cell and answered. "Daniel?"

"He's home," Daniel replied.

"Thank God." Benny's hold on the steering wheel loosened. "Is he okay?"

"Yeah. He has a few scratches on his arms and legs because he came in through the woods to bypass the press, but they're nothing some peroxide won't fix."

"Is it okay if I check for myself? I'm a block away." Benny held his breath, praying Jamie would see him.

"Yeah, I think that'd be a good idea. Tony's got him in the bathroom, taking care of his wounds. He knows his father's here, but he hasn't made a move to see him."

Benny shook his head as he passed the same news van that had disrupted the pool party. The other news outlets came and went, but that persistent sonofabitch was refusing to give up until he got his story. Benny had a feeling the reporter—who he'd discovered was Bob Keen from one of the local networks—was carrying a grudge for the way he'd been manhandled off Tony's driveway several weeks earlier. Whatever the reason, Mr. Keen had become a permanent fixture in front of the house.

Benny pulled up the long driveway and parked his beat-up Chevy next to the black limousine that had to belong to Jamie's father. "Pretentious prick."

Benny had done some light research on Jamie's father after the first weekend they'd spent together. Senator Whitmore was a real piece of work. Benny had watched several videotaped speeches of Whitmore practically declaring war on the LGBT community. With all the senator's talk of homosexuals destroying the fabric of America, it was no wonder the press wanted to find out whether or not Whitmore had known his son was gay.

Pocketing his keys, Benny approached the front of the house. If Jamie's father was waiting by the pool, Benny could get inside without the man knowing Jamie's backup had arrived. And, if Jamie didn't want to speak to his father at all, Benny would be more than happy to get rid of the asshole.

Daniel opened the door and ushered Benny inside. "Tony just finished with Jamie. I hope you don't mind, but I told Jamie you were coming in case he didn't want to see you."

"What'd he say?" Benny asked. He knew he had a huge apology to make, but first they needed to deal with the senator.

"Not much, but he didn't tell us to keep you away from him, so I guess that's a good sign." Daniel led the way into the living room. "Where's Jamie?" he asked Tony.

Tony finished pouring a drink before nodding toward the kitchen. "I think he's gathering his nerve to face his dad."

Daniel pushed Benny toward the kitchen. "Go and fix this."

Benny did as Daniel had ordered. When he entered the kitchen, he found Jamie sitting at the table with his head in his hands. "Hey."

Jamie glanced up before resuming his original position. "What're you doing here?"

Benny took in the scrapes and scratches on Jamie's arms as he sat beside him. "I came to tell you what a fuckwad I am, and to beg for your forgiveness."

Jamie looked up at Benny again. "Do people who are nothing but casual sex partners beg for forgiveness?"

"No," Benny said, but that was all he was willing to admit. He reached over and lifted Jamie out of the chair before settling him on his lap. "I had a bad day, and I took it out on you for no other reason than you were there. When what I should have been grateful for was that you were there in the first place."

"Yeah," Jamie agreed.

"Why'd you run out like that if you didn't have a ride home?" Benny asked. "Pissed or not, I could've given you a lift."

Jamie sighed and leaned his head against Benny's shoulder. "I was so angry that I didn't realize I had no way to get home until after I'd already stormed out." He shrugged. "I was too embarrassed to go back in and ask. I did okay until I got close to the house and remembered the reporter. I didn't want to deal with him, so I came in through the rear of the house."

Benny held Jamie for several moments before bringing up the elephant in the room, or in their case, the elephant by the pool. "What do you want to do about your dad? Say the word, and I'll get rid of him."

"Thanks, but I'll have to talk to him. I was just sitting here gathering my courage."

"You want me to go out there with you?" Benny didn't want to intrude on Jamie's personal business, but he needed him to know he'd have his back if necessary.

"No thanks. Dad would probably have a heart attack if my big black lover got in his face." Jamie grinned. "Actually, now that I think about it..." His smile died as his voice trailed off. "You don't deserve the kind of shit that man can dish out." He gave Benny a soft kiss before climbing off his lap. "Do me a favor and keep an eye on us through the window. If he or his driver tries to shove me in the limo, rescue me."

"I won't let anything happen to you," Benny said, meaning every word.

* * * *

Jamie took a deep breath and squared his shoulders before approaching his father. "You wanted to see me?"

Everett looked up from his phone and scowled. "It's about time. Where've you been?"

"None of your business." Jamie leaned his hip against the table his father was seated at. "Did you think you could change my mind by browbeating me in person?"

Everett reached into the inside pocket of his suit. "The private detective I hired to follow you sent me these." He withdrew a folded envelope. "It seems you've been busy." He held it out toward Jamie.

Jamie stared at his father. "You've had me followed?"

"Of course," Everett replied with no hint of apology in his tone. "I'm not sure why you find this so difficult to understand, but what you do has a direct effect on my business. Thus, you and your private life are, and always will be, my business."

"Thus? Seriously? Who uses words like that?" Jamie snatched the envelope out of his father's hand. "I can't imagine what your private dick could've found since I've barely been off this property since I arrived." He opened the envelope and withdrew a small stack of photos.

Pictures in hand, Jamie moved closer to one of the landscaping lights. There were two pictures of him and Daniel lounging beside the pool in their swimsuits, and four of him and Benny. One of the photos caught his attention, but not for the reason they were taken. It was a picture of him with Benny's arm around him as they walked from the pottery shed to the house. Jamie's love for Benny was right there for anyone to see. *Damn.* At the time, he hadn't noticed the soft expression on Benny's handsome face as he looked down at him. Benny could believe what he wanted, but the photo was proof that he had feelings for Jamie that didn't have anything to do with casual sex.

"Can I keep these?" Jamie asked.

"Is that all you have to say?" Everett's chest puffed out as he stalked toward Jamie. "Are you fucking those men?"

"Again, not that it's any of your business, but Daniel is my landlord." Jamie held up the picture with Daniel in it before flashing the one with Benny. "This is the man who is fucking me. What other details would you like? Do you want to know which positions I prefer or how big his cock is? I'll share that information with you if you call off your private detective."

"Don't be disgusting!" Everett bellowed. "This is a very serious situation. It's one thing for you to proclaim you're gay, but to shove your deviant lifestyle into people's faces is not acceptable for a son of mine."

"Aaarghhh," Jamie growled with his head tipped back. He couldn't believe his father was so self-absorbed. "First of all, I'm not shoving anything in people's faces." He held up the photos. "These were taken on private property by a man you fucking hired! Secondly, I don't need or care what you consider acceptable anymore. To me, *you're* not acceptable. To me, *you're* a bigoted asshole who thinks all is fine between you and God as long as you only fuck your *female* interns."

The slap that landed hard against Jamie's cheek knocked him off balance, sending Jamie to the pavement. "Shut up!" Everett screamed.

Jamie's heart and mind reeled with what had just taken place. Never in his life had his father hit him.

"Get out!" Benny yelled as he came storming onto the patio.

Jamie couldn't say a word as Benny walked straight to Everett and bumped him with his muscular chest. "Get in your fancy-assed ride and get the fuck outta here," Benny growled in Everett's face as he continued to nudge him backward.

Red with anger, Everett tried to stand his ground. "No nigger's going to tell me what to do."

Benny's hands curled into fists. "I swear to God, man, you're two seconds away from feeling the full effects of this *nigger's* wrath."

Everett broke away from Benny before turning his hateful gaze on Jamie. "Do something about your pet monkey," he demanded.

Benny reared back to, no doubt, punch the senator in the face, when Jamie finally snapped out of his stupor.

"Stop!" Jamie shouted as he got to his feet. He moved to put himself between Benny and Everett. Although he would've been happy to let Benny loose on his father, Jamie knew it would only land Benny in a world of lawsuits and criminal charges. Nope. There was only one thing his father understood.

"If you're not in your car by the time I count to three, I'm going to march my deviant ass down the driveway and spill my guts to the reporter about what kind of man you really are. Is that what you want, *Father*?"

"No need for all that," Tony said from the darkness. "I decided to invite Bob and his friend Jeff to a pool party."

It was then that Jamie spotted Bob Keen and his camera operator. Both men had huge smiles on their faces. "Best party I've ever been invited to," Keen said.

* * * *

Benny helped Jamie into bed before sitting beside him. He'd forgotten all about his meeting with Chase and needed to call him, but first, he needed to get Jamie settled. "I'm going to ask Daniel if he has anything to put on your cheek." He leaned down and kissed Jamie's forehead, hoping Jamie would forgive him for also sending a message to Chase while he was gone. "Need anything while I'm up?"

"Would you check to see if they're gone?" Jamie asked.

"Sure, babe." Benny handed Jamie the television remote before leaving the bedroom. He walked out of the pool house, surprised to find it was finally quiet.

After discovering his tirade had been videotaped, the senator had immediately gone into damage-control mode. At first he'd tried to get the footage back by claiming it was a private family matter and not newsworthy. When that hadn't worked, he'd threatened the local station with a lawsuit if they released the tape or spoke about the incident.

Benny wasn't sure how it had turned out because he'd swiftly led Jamie into the pool house. He couldn't put his finger on it, but the slap had seemed to do more damage to Jamie than bruise his cheek. Benny couldn't blame Jamie for the way he felt. He couldn't imagine his own dad talking to him the way the senator had spoken to Jamie.

Benny spotted a faint red glow off to his left when he opened his car door. "Who's there?"

"Just me," Tony replied, taking another drag from his cigarette.

Benny retrieved his phone before shutting the door. "I didn't know you smoked."

"I don't do it very often around Daniel, but I needed one tonight." Tony gestured to the pool house. "How's he doing?"

"Hard to say. I told him I'd get something for his face, but I don't think that's what's hurting him at the moment," Benny explained.

"I reckon not," Tony agreed. "I respect the way you stood up for him. It's hard to believe you're only eighteen, because you hold yourself like a man when it's needed."

"Thanks. I fuck up a lot, but I have a good role model on how a man should act. How Jamie learned to be the man he is I have no idea, because his father's a complete jackass." Benny sent a mental reminder to call his dad in the morning.

Tony stubbed his cigarette out in a potted plant next to the house. "Shhh," he whispered. "Don't tell Daniel."

"Wouldn't dream of it," Benny agreed.

Tony started back to the door but stopped before opening it. "As long as you treat him right, you're welcome to stay here."

"I appreciate that." Benny watched as Tony gave him a single nod before disappearing into the house. Benny wasted no time sending Chase a text.

Sorry I missed our meeting. Jamie had some trouble that he needed help with. By the time I remembered the meeting, it was too late to call.

The back door opened again and Tony walked out, holding a bag of frozen peas. He tossed it to Benny. "Put this on Jamie's cheek."

"Thanks." Benny's phone chimed and he glanced down at the screen.

Don't worry about it. Glad you were there for him. We'll talk later.

Feeling better about clearing the air with Chase, Benny shoved the phone into his pocket. He entered the pool house with one goal in mind — comforting Jamie. "Tony found me a bag of frozen peas," he announced as he opened the bedroom door.

"I'm not hungry."

Smiling, Benny kicked off his shoes. "They're for your face, not your stomach." He tossed the bag to Jamie then stripped down to his underwear. "Anything good on TV?" he asked as he crawled into bed and gathered Jamie in his arms.

"I don't know. I've been trolling news channels, expecting to see one of the most humiliating moments of my life broadcast for the whole world to see."

Benny took the peas out of Jamie's hand. "These have to be on the actual bruise in order for them to do their job." He gently pressed the bag against Jamie's cheek. "I know it's a dick thing for me to say, but I'm lucky there was no one around to tape my humiliation on the stairs today. I can't imagine what that must feel like."

Jamie snuggled closer to Benny. "He hit me."

"Yeah. I'm sorry I didn't get out there in time to stop it from happening." Benny would never forget the sight of the much bigger senator knocking his son to the ground with one powerful blow to the face. He'd listened to Chase's stories about his abusive father, and he thought he'd understood what his boyfriend, at the time, had gone through as a child. It took today's scenario to make him realize that he'd had no real clue what Chase had suffered. Once again, Benny made a mental note to reach out to his own father.

"It's not your fault. Growing up, my father couldn't be bothered to discipline me." Jamie looked up at Benny. "He left that to Mom, and she was a softie who believed in time outs and shit like that." He shrugged. "I always thought my father was just too busy to deal with stuff like that, but I'm beginning to think he never liked me. Maybe he sensed I was different than the other boys in my class. Who knows? Anyway, the point I'm trying to make is that the slap you saw was the first time I can remember my father even touching me since I was young. He's never been the kind of dad who mussed my hair or slapped me on the back when I did something he approved of. Like I said, he's always been indifferent toward me."

"First break we get from school, I want to take you back to Cattle Valley with me, so I can show you what a real dad is like." Benny smiled just thinking about his dad. "After my mom died, we had a few years where we didn't get along, but he never stopped trying to break down the walls I'd built between us."

"Why'd you build the walls in the first place?" Jamie asked, removing the cold pack from his cheek.

"Several reasons. I hated that he moved us to Cattle Valley. I hated the way he looked at men. He never really came out to me until I was older and started to have feelings for Chase, but I knew he was different by the way he acted with Pete. He tried to tell me he and Pete were just friends because they worked together at the Sheriff's Department, but I'd catch them looking at each other or holding hands. But, I think more than anything, after my mom died, I realized how much it hurt to lose someone I loved, so I decided it would be better if I just stopped loving him.

He had a dangerous job, and I knew he risked his life every time he left the house in his uniform. I didn't want to hurt again the way I'd hurt with Mom."

The way I'd hurt when Chase left me.

"I'd like to meet him," Jamie said. "Too bad classes start on Monday. I would've suggested a road trip."

"They bought season tickets to the games, so you'll get to meet him here in a couple weeks, but he won't act the same as he does at home." Benny cupped Jamie's face and rubbed the pad of his thumb across the blossoming bruise. "Although I'm sorry your dad hurt you, I'm sorrier that I did."

Turning his head, Jamie captured Benny's thumb between his lips and began to suck.

Benny groaned. As much as he wanted to roll over on top of Jamie and fuck until they both forgot about everything and everyone but each other, he needed to prove something to Jamie even more. Regretfully, he pulled his thumb from Jamie's mouth. "Can we just hold each other tonight?"

Jamie's eyes rounded at the request. "Are you sore from the stairs?"

Benny decided to go with that excuse. "Yeah, babe. I'd like to go rummage in your kitchen for something to eat, watch mindless television and hold you. Is that okay with you?"

Jamie nodded. "I made lasagna for Daniel, Tony and I. Want some?"

Benny's stomach growled at the mention of one of his favorite foods. "I may just worship you forever for a piece of that."

"Then what am I waiting for?" Jamie slid out of bed. He opened his dresser drawer and pulled out a pair of shorts. "Although it's not late, I'm going to text Daniel to let him know I'm sneaking into the kitchen." He dressed quickly before picking up his phone. "After everything that happened, he's probably on edge."

Benny leaned up on his forearm. "He seemed fine earlier."

"Yeah, but he was probably running on adrenaline. Now that things have calmed down, the ghosts from his past might haunt him for a few hours."

Benny wanted to ask what had happened to Daniel, but he decided not to pry. "You don't have to bother them. I can have lasagna for breakfast."

Jamie walked around to Benny's side of the bed. "My man needs food." He leaned over and kissed Benny. "So I'm going to get him a big plate of the lasagna I made."

Benny watched Jamie leave the room, unsure of how to react to being labeled as Jamie's man. He supposed it had a lot to do with his unresolved feelings for Chase. Maybe, after he'd had a chance to sit down and talk to Chase, he'd have a better idea of how attached to him he could let Jamie become. *Fuck!* He felt like he was only half living in two worlds.

Chapter Six

Jamie woke early the following morning and smiled at the loud snores coming from the man beside him. Most people complained when their partners snored, but Jamie found the sound comforting. Even in sleep, the constant reminder that he wasn't alone soothed him.

Rolling to his side, he repositioned the pillow under his bruised cheek so he could watch Benny snooze for as long as possible. He was crazy for falling in love with someone so young. He remembered how crazy he'd gone his freshman year of college. For the first time in his life, he'd had the freedom to fuck random guys without his parents watching his every move. Part of him believed Benny deserved the same experiences. After all, how realistic was it for him to expect Benny to settle down at the age of eighteen?

The second Benny stopped snoring, Jamie shut his eyes and tried to even his breaths. The last thing he wanted was to be caught ogling.

Benny reached for Jamie. "Morning," Benny mumbled.

"How'd you know I was awake?" Jamie asked.

"Because you weren't snoring."

Jamie opened his eyes and stared at Benny. "I don't snore."

Benny chuckled. "The hell you don't. It may not be as loud as mine, but you snuffle when you sleep." He rubbed his nose against Jamie's. "Don't worry. I think it's cute."

Jamie groaned. "Lovely."

When Benny moved to insinuate himself between Jamie's thighs, it was his turn to groan. "Fuck, I'm sore." He closed his eyes and touched his forehead to Jamie's. "I wanted to fuck you this morning, but I think it might kill me."

Jamie wrapped his arms around Benny and spent a moment simply holding him. "I'll make you a deal. You try to stop saying fuck all the time, and I'll give you a massage."

Benny chuckled. "Only if you'll promise not to tell my dad about my cussing habit when you meet him. Growing up, I made my dad put money in the swear jar every time he said a bad word. I earned enough to buy a ten-speed bike before he got his mouth under control."

"So you're saying I need to get a swear jar?" Jamie decided to make one at his first opportunity.

"Don't forget I'm a poor college student. You have to give me at least five free passes a day," Benny said.

"Five? Hmm." Jamie pretended to consider Benny's offer. "Okay, how's this? Any use of the word fuck outside of talking about actually fucking, and I'll make you pay up."

"So..." Benny paused for effect. "Only the word fuck is punishable?"

Jamie narrowed his eyes. "Yes. Although, you absolutely cannot start substituting other swear words for that one."

After a moment, Benny nodded before moving to stretch out on his stomach. "Deal. Massage away."

Satisfied by their arrangement, Jamie climbed out of bed. He didn't have massage oil, but he did have lotion. At the last second, he grabbed the bottle of lube. After all, the fun in giving another man a massage was access to every single inch of him.

"Should I start with your legs?" Jamie asked as he knelt beside Benny's prostrate body.

Benny answered without lifting his face from the pillow. "As long as you finish with my cock."

"Oh, don't worry about that." Jamie poured lotion into his hand. "You want the lotion warm or cold?"

"Warm," Benny mumbled.

Jamie rubbed his hands together for several moments before placing them on Benny's ankles. With a firm touch, he ran his palms up the backs of Benny's legs. When he reached Benny's butt, he took a moment to rub the twin muscular globes. God, Benny had a great ass.

Too soon, he needed to stop touching Benny to gather more lotion. "Okay, this isn't going to work for me. The lotion just soaks into your skin too fast. Mind if I use lube?"

"I don't care what you use as long as you put your hands back on me," Benny replied.

"Right." Jamie held the bottle of lube over Benny's naked body. "I'm not warming it, so brace yourself." He dripped a line from ankle to shoulder on both sides before closing the cap. "My sheets'll probably be trashed by the time we're done."

"Probably," Benny agreed.

"Shit. What if it soaks through to the mattress?" Jamie chewed on his bottom lip as he pondered the situation.

Benny stuck his ass in the air and wiggled his hips from side to side, drawing Jamie's attention.

"Yeah, fuck the mattress," Jamie said.

"Language," Benny admonished.

"Patience." Jamie grinned as he leaned over and lightly bit Benny's butt cheek. He wanted to concentrate on that ass, but he'd promised a massage, so he set to work.

By the time Jamie had thoroughly worked Benny's calves and thighs, he was practically panting. He gathered more lube on his hands before moving to straddle Benny's legs. "This okay?"

"Mmm hmm," came the muffled reply.

Jamie began to rub Benny's ass. With each stroke upward, he worked his thumbs closer and closer to Benny's puckered hole. In the weeks that they'd been together, he'd never asked to top Benny because he'd so enjoyed the feel of Benny's cock inside him, but when Benny reached back to separate the cheeks of his ass, Jamie got the feeling he'd done a disservice to his partner.

Jamie coated Benny's pucker with lube before slowly pushing the tip of his thumb inside. He held his breath as he waited for Benny's reaction to the invasion.

"Can I say fuck?" Benny asked.

Jamie chuckled. "By all means."

"Fuck," Benny growled as Jamie sank further inside him.

As tight as Benny was, Jamie wondered if he'd ever been breached. Unfortunately, he knew from previous conversations that Benny had only been with Chase, and asking questions about Benny's sex life with Chase wasn't going to happen.

"Condom," Benny ordered, his voice gruff with need.

Nodding enthusiastically, Jamie reached for the bedside table. He dug in the drawer and came out with the box he'd originally purchased. He shook it, hoping there was at least one left, and was rewarded when two condoms spilled into his hand. Unfortunately, when he tried to open the package, he found his hands were too slippery.

Jamie passed the condom to Benny. "Open this."

Benny tore open the foil wrapper with his teeth, grimacing at the taste of the lube on his tongue. "Here."

"Thanks." Jamie rolled the rubber down his erection. He remembered how tight the condom was on Benny's cock and felt inadequate when the latex slid down without difficulty. It sucked because he'd never considered his dick small, but it was puny compared to Benny's.

Benny reached out and put his hand on Jamie's. "Stop it. You're perfect the way you are."

Jamie met Benny's gaze. "I just want it to be good for you."

Benny licked his lips. "I've never wanted it like I do at this minute. That should tell you something."

It did and it didn't, Jamie decided. It still didn't answer the question as to whether or not Benny had ever been fucked, so Jamie decided to go as slow as possible. He knelt behind Benny, who had already positioned his knees under himself, and directed the head of his cock to Benny's hole. Benny's muscles quivered slightly when Jamie pushed his crown inside. He paused, afraid he was hurting the man he'd come to care about.

"Just tell me when you're ready for more," Jamie instructed.

Instead of answering Jamie, Benny pushed back against Jamie's erection, pushing a few more inches inside.

Goosebumps broke out on Benny's chocolate brown skin, and Jamie couldn't help but give in to his need to soothe. He ran his palm down Benny's spine. "Don't force it if it hurts. I want it to be good."

"It's beyond good, babe. It's more than I'd ever thought it could be." Benny looked over his shoulder. "Give me more."

Jamie leaned in, burying himself slowly until he was sheathed to the hilt inside Benny.

"You can move," Benny said.

Jamie bit the inside of his cheek to distract himself. "Not yet. Be patient with me for a second. I don't want this to be over before it gets started."

Benny nodded. "Did I tell you my roommate's a nudist?"

Jamie's focus went from the feel of Benny's ass squeezing his shaft to the question that had come from left field. "What?"

"My roommate, Twitch. Apparently, he was raised in a nudist colony. I've been trying to imagine what it would be like to see my dad's and everyone else's junk all the time." Benny turned and grinned at Jamie. "If that's not enough to distract you so you can fuck me, nothing is."

Jamie tried to picture sitting down to dinner nude with his parents and shivered. "Yeah, that's a deflator more than a distraction."

Benny started to laugh and the movement of his body created a delicious ache in Jamie's groin. He pulled his cock from Benny before sliding back inside. Benny's moan of approval spurred Jamie into action. He gripped Benny's hips and repeated the motion, surging in harder with each thrust.

"I'm coming!" Benny yelled, grinding his ass against Jamie.

Thank God. Jamie held his orgasm in check for three more strokes before he let himself go. The climax that rocked through him sapped every ounce of energy from his body. He collapsed on Benny's back and struggled to breathe.

Benny dropped to the mattress and the two of them lay in silence for several minutes. "I had no idea what I was missing out on," Benny mumbled.

Jamie smiled, pleased he could give that gift to Benny. "Are we going to have a fight every time we get in bed over who has to top now?"

"No. I love burying my dick inside you." Benny rose up until Jamie got the hint and slid off him. After Jamie rid himself of the condom, Benny gathered Jamie in his arms and kissed him.

Grabbing the back of Benny's head, Jamie took the kiss deeper. He was so lost in the taste of Benny that he jumped when his phone on the dresser began to play Daniel's familiar ringtone.

Benny broke their lip lock and narrowed his gaze at the intrusion.

"Sorry, but I should get that. Daniel wouldn't call this early unless it was important." Jamie was out of bed before he realized his hands were still slick with lube. He grabbed the sheet and pulled, uncovering Benny's flaccid penis. "Nice," he noted as he wiped his hands.

By the time he was clean enough to handle his phone, it had stopped ringing, so he called Daniel. "What's up?" he asked when Daniel answered.

"I just thought I'd give you a heads-up. The video aired on every news outlet in the country overnight. Evidently, Bob Keen wasn't going to take the chance of your father using his position to bury it. Needless to say, the cops are already out front trying to direct traffic. I swear, it must be a slow news day because there are at least a hundred reporters jockeying for position in front of the house."

"Shit. Is Tony mad?" Jamie would completely understand if Tony asked him to move out.

"At you? Hell no. He's pissed off at himself for believing that if Bob Keen got his story, it would put an end to your father's bid for re-election, therefore ending the press's interest in you. He just wanted you to be able to live a normal life without fear of a reporter sticking a microphone in your face." Daniel sighed. "His plan backfired. From what we've seen on the news, your father must've paid Keen and his cameraman off because the video they're showing has definitely been recut. Instead of putting your father in a bad light, it makes it seem as though you're a spoiled brat who loves to shove his lifestyle in his conservative father's face. Your dad's more popular than he's ever been."

"What about the slap? Does it show him knocking me to the ground?" Jamie asked, feeling sick to his stomach.

"No. It shows you talking about Benny and the fact that he's fucking you. It does show your father telling you to shut up, but then it cuts to Benny coming out of the house to get in your father's face. Everett's racial slurs are even cut out."

Jamie wasn't even aware he'd sunk to the floor until Benny picked him up and carried him back to bed. Benny took the phone out of Jamie's hand.

"This is Benny," Benny said into the cell. "Yeah. Okay, I'll see what I can do. See you in a few." He hung up. "Daniel wants us to come over. He's making a big breakfast so we can come up with a plan."

Jamie wiggled his way out of Benny's lap. "I'm going to take a shower."

"I'll come with you," Benny offered.

Jamie held up his hand. "Thanks, but I need a minute alone."

"Okay," Benny conceded.

Still in a daze, Jamie stumbled to the bathroom. He didn't care that his personal life was out there for everyone to ridicule because, despite everything, he wasn't ashamed of who he was, but Benny didn't deserve the negative press. It wasn't even the chance that the information could harm Benny's dream of playing pro ball. After all, there weren't many players out and proud on the football field. No. The fact was, Benny was only eighteen. He had his whole life to prove to himself and the world around him what kind of man he was, and with one snippet of film, Benny's name would be forever tainted by the scandal. Even if people forgot the news story, that video would be on the internet, hounding him, until the day he died.

Jamie turned on the water and stepped under the spray before it had a chance to heat up. He knew in his heart that once Benny realized what had happened, he'd cut all ties to him. "Fuck!" he screamed, using Benny's favorite word.

* * * *

After Jamie had walked out of the room, Benny reached for the remote. He didn't know what Daniel had told Jamie, but it had been clear it had to do with the situation the previous evening. Flipping to one of the twenty-four-hour news channels, he turned the volume down low enough for him to hear without the sound disturbing Jamie's shower.

Rage filled him when he caught the top story. The video the station showed was a fucking lie. Unable to breathe at the injustice, he dug his phone out of his pocket. When he turned it on, he wasn't surprised to see half a dozen missed calls from his dad.

He pulled on his shorts before reaching out to his dad.

"Shit, Benny, I've been going crazy. How are you?" Brian asked.

"Not good," Benny admitted. "I'm so pissed off that I don't know where to direct my anger."

"You can start by taking a deep breath and telling me what happened."

Benny decided to get out of the house while he spoke to his father. The last thing he wanted was for Jamie to overhear his anger toward Everett Whitmore and everything the man stood for. "Hang on."

Benny slipped out and sat at one of the lounge chairs beside the pool. He started from the beginning, telling his dad everything—how he'd met Jamie, how long they'd been seeing each other, and finally about the previous night's altercation with Senator Whitmore.

"Damn, son," Brian said when Benny finished. "Damn," he repeated.

"Yeah," Benny agreed. "I really care about him, Dad, but I don't know how to fix this."

"You don't have to fix it. This isn't your fault. It isn't Jamie's fault. Unfortunately, the best thing you can do for him is to be there for him until all this dies down."

Benny heard Pete's voice in the background. "What's Pete saying?"

"That he called the station to clear a few days off. We're going to head that way," Brian replied.

"You guys don't have to do that, Dad."

"Yes we do. We're not about to let the two of you go through this alone. Even if all we can do is protect you from the press, it'll make us feel better," Brian said. "Given stops for Ethan's small bladder, we should be there in ten hours or so. Keep your phone on you."

Despite what he'd said, Benny was grateful his dad, Pete and Ethan were coming. He wanted to be strong for Jamie, but wasn't sure he had the skills to deal with the situation on his own, and while he appreciated Daniel and Tony's help, they weren't family. Before the run-in with Jamie's father, the biggest issues he'd ever dealt with were the loss of his mom, the realization he was gay and the break-up with Chase, all three of which he'd handled with anger, and not successfully. The rage coursing through his system on Jamie's behalf scared him.

"You saw the video, didn't you?"

Benny looked up to see Jamie standing just outside the pool house door. "Yeah," he admitted.

Jamie began to worry his bottom lip with his teeth. "I'm sorry you've been dragged into this."

Benny tried like hell to push down his anger. He got to his feet and held out his hand. "You've nothing to be sorry for. Let's go see what Daniel's made us for breakfast."

Chapter Seven

Benny glanced at the time on his cell phone. His dad should be here any minute, and he couldn't help but feel nervous. He, Jamie, Tony, Daniel and Tony's lawyer Vince, had come up with a plan of attack, but everyone had agreed to wait and make the final decision after talking it over with Benny's dad.

"Truck just pulled in," Tony announced, coming into the living room. "You feel like doing this in here or would it be easier in the kitchen?"

"Kitchen. They'll probably be hungry," Benny replied. He called Jamie, who had gone with Daniel to the studio to release some anxiety.

"Hey," Jamie answered.

"Hey, babe. How're you doing?" Benny asked.

"Well, after I broke my second vase, Daniel told me to grab a broom and start sweeping up instead. Are they here?"

"Yep. They just pulled in." It hadn't been easy for Benny to let Jamie go to the studio without him, even if it was only a hundred yards from the house, but he figured it was best for both of them to spend a few hours apart. However, now that he had his anger under control, he couldn't wait to see Jamie again. "Will you tell Daniel? We're meeting in the kitchen so they can sample your cooking."

Benny heard his father's voice and smiled. "Gotta go give my dad a hug. Hurry and get here."

"Okay," Jamie replied before ending the call.

Benny found the group making introductions in the large foyer. "You made it," he said as he wrapped his arms around his dad.

Brian held Benny in his fatherly embrace for several moments before releasing him. He planted his hands on Benny's shoulders and looked Benny in the eyes. "How're you holding up?"

"Better," Benny admitted. He turned to Pete and Ethan who were standing just out of arm's reach. In the years that he'd known the two men, he'd rarely shown either of them affection, but their willingness to drop everything and come to his aid had touched something deep inside him. He wasted no time in pulling Pete then Ethan into a quick, back-pounding embrace. "Thanks for coming. I know you didn't have to."

Ethan stared up at Benny. "Of course we came, we're your family."

Benny's throat thickened as his eyes filled with tears at Ethan's truthful sentiment. He knew he was lucky. He had three men who were looking out for his best interests while Jamie's own father seemed hell-bent on destroying his only son for the sake of his career.

"Why don't we go into the kitchen," Tony suggested.

"That sounds good," Brian answered.

"You hungry? Jamie and Benny prepared a pan of chicken enchiladas," Tony said as they walked through the dining room.

Brian glanced over his shoulder at Benny. "You cooked?"

"Please," Benny scoffed and shook his head. "I cut up the tomatoes and shredded the cheese."

Brian returned his attention to Tony. "If Benny didn't cook them, we'll definitely have some."

The back door opened and Jamie stood there, panting and looking unsure of himself.

"Where's Daniel?" Tony asked.

Jamie hooked his thumb over his shoulder. "Behind me somewhere," he replied in a voice so soft Benny barely heard him.

Benny walked over to Jamie and gave him a smile before wrapping his arm around Jamie's trim waist. "Dad, Pete, Ethan, this is Jamie." He felt proud to introduce the adults he cared about to the man who was quickly becoming the most important person in his world.

When Brian stepped forward, Jamie broke away from Benny and held out his hand. Brian shook his head and gathered Jamie into his arms. "I'm a hugger," Brian said. "Sorry, but you'll have to get used to it."

Jamie nodded, but when he started to step back, Brian pulled him in even tighter. He said something in Jamie's ear that Benny couldn't hear and suddenly Jamie was hugging him back.

By the time they'd released each other, Jamie's eyes had filled with tears. He quickly blinked the moisture away before shaking Pete's and Ethan's hands.

Benny eased his arm around Jamie once more. He bent to whisper in Jamie's ear. "Okay?"

Jamie tipped his head back and gave Benny a smile. "I'm good."

Satisfied that his dad hadn't done permanent damage, Benny started to lead Jamie to the kitchen table while his dad, Ethan and Pete filled their plates.

"Wait," Jamie said, tugging his hand from Benny's. "I need a bottle of water. You?"

"Sure." Benny took a seat just as Daniel walked into the room. He watched the six men and hoped Jamie understood that he was no longer alone in his fight against his father.

The doorbell rang and everyone stopped what they were doing.

"That's probably my guy," Tony said, leaving the room.

Daniel looked to Benny. "Tony has a guy?"

Benny grinned. "I think he's talking about the man from the security company."

Daniel pressed a hand to his chest. "Thank God. I thought I was gonna have to go all crazy on him in front of company."

If someone had told Benny a month ago that he'd spend his time hanging out with men old enough to be his father, he'd have called them crazy. He was starting to realize that after you reached a certain point in your life, age didn't matter as much as it once had. He thought of the age difference between Chase and Mac. Benny had been disgusted that Chase could fall for a man so much older, but the more time he spent with Daniel and Tony, the more he understood it.

By the time Tony came back into the room with a laptop, everyone except Daniel, who was still milling around, was seated at the table. "Brian, before we start, I think you, Pete and Ethan should watch this.

It's the security footage from last night. We watched the feed earlier, but it was a little fuzzy, so I had someone clean it up as much as he could. Unfortunately, it doesn't have sound, but I think it's clear to see the tape released to the media was creatively edited."

Benny tucked Jamie close to his side as the others watched the video. Several times, Brian's gaze met Benny's over the laptop, but Benny wasn't sure what his dad was thinking. Ethan jerked at one point and both Brian and Pete put their arms around him. Benny knew a little about Ethan's past, so he assumed it was the part in the video where Everett had slapped Jamie.

Brian closed the laptop and blew out a long breath before looking at Jamie. "I don't know what to say other than no one deserves to be treated like that by a parent."

"I've got something to say," Pete began. "You need to show this to the local cops and have your dad charged with assault."

"That's the first thing we plan to do with the footage," Benny said. "Jamie and I talked about it, and we think it might be a good idea to release the uncut video to the press. We may not be able to prove Senator Whitmore said those things to us, but, like Tony said, at least it proves the tape the networks received had been doctored."

Brian reached across the table and clasped Jamie's hand. "Have you thought of the repercussions involved? I don't know anything about your mom or if you have brothers or sisters, but this might damage your relationship with them beyond repair. It's never easy to air family laundry, but for what it's worth, I think you should consider those things first. There's nothing wrong with releasing this to the police—in fact, I'd suggest it. If charges are filed and they pick up your father, the press will get wind of it anyway. Maybe that's the best way to get the truth out there. You can give the police permission to share the video with the press, but it won't be you doing it. Does that make sense?"

Jamie nodded. "I don't think it'll do any good to talk to my mom, but I suppose she deserves to make her own decision on who to stand behind."

"I think you're probably right," Brian agreed. He turned his attention to Benny. "I'm proud of you, son, for standing up to someone in Everett's position. I know it couldn't have been easy."

"You're wrong, Dad. It killed me not to do something before the senator ever struck Jamie, but when I saw that, I didn't care who the man was. My only concern was for Jamie." Benny pulled Jamie even closer to his side. The way it was going, Jamie would be sitting on his lap before they finished the conversation.

"Another thing to consider," Tony began, "is contacting an attorney. Since we can prove that footage was altered before being released to the press, you both have a valid case for a defamation suit against Everett, Bob Keen, the cameraman and the station Bob represents."

"I don't want to sue anyone," Jamie replied.

"Don't be too quick to make that decision," Tony urged. "My guess is that if you name either the cameraman or Bob Keen in a lawsuit, they are going to try and settle. The best thing for the two of you would be for the original footage to be released, which I think you could do with a minimal amount of pressure from a top team of attorneys.

"I don't have the money for a lawyer," Jamie admitted. "I barely have enough to get me through school and to tide me over until I can sell some of my work."

"I'll be more than happy to have my team of attorneys represent you and Benny. However, with the television station and your father, I think you should go after a monetary judgment against them," Tony said.

Benny exchanged glances with Jamie before looking to his dad. "What do you think?"

Brian crossed his arms over his chest. "You know how I feel about frivolous lawsuits, but in this case, I don't believe there's anything frivolous at all. We can hope pressing charges and getting the truth out there clears both your names but there's no guarantee of that. What the senator has done has put your future in the pros, if it comes to that, in jeopardy."

Jamie slid out of his chair. "I think I need to call my mom." He gestured to the laptop. "You can go ahead and call the cops," he told Tony.

"Okay," Tony agreed.

"You want me to go with you?" Benny asked.

Jamie shook his head. "I think this is something I need to do on my own."

Benny reached for Jamie's hand and gave it a squeeze. "I'll be right here if you need me."

Food forgotten, Brian rose and looked at Benny. "Why don't we go somewhere and talk?"

"Is it okay if we use the living room?" Benny asked Tony.

"Sure," Tony replied.

Benny led the way into the comfortable but expensively decorated formal living room. He wasn't sure what his dad wanted to talk about, but he was nervous about the impending conversation. Before Benny had a chance to sit, Brian pulled him into one of his famous bear hugs.

"I don't think I've ever been more proud of you. It breaks my heart what Jamie's going through, and I just wanted you to know how much I love you, and that nothing you can ever do will change that."

Benny leaned back when he heard tears in his dad's voice. His dad rarely cried, so the sight of the emotion clearly written on his face and in his words stunned Benny. "I feel the same way about you, Dad. We may have had our differences in the past, but never for a second did I ever feel unloved or unwanted."

With a strong pat on Benny's back, Brian released him. "Now, sit down and tell me about Jamie."

Benny took a seat on the sofa. "I already told you about him when we spoke on the phone."

"No, you gave me a timetable of events and told me you cared for him, but I want to know what it is you see in him." Brian moved several toss pillows until he was comfortable.

"What do you mean what I see in him? Dad, you were just in the same room with him. Okay, maybe you haven't had the chance to see how funny he is and how much he makes me laugh, but surely you could see what a good person he is. I mean, his initial reaction to suing people who have hurt him to the bone was no. That's because he has a huge heart. I can't wait for you to see his work. He gave me one of his vases, and I've never seen anything more beautiful in my life. It's like he creates these fine works of art out of a lump of clay." Once Benny started, everything came pouring out. "When I talk to him, he really listens, and when he touches me, I can't imagine ever being happy again without his warmth on my body."

Benny's face heated when he realized what he'd just admitted. "Sorry."

Brian grinned. "Don't be. I don't know how you managed to fall so completely in love so fast, but I've no doubt you've done it because everything you've just said is the way I feel about Ethan and Pete. And, I don't mean to bring up a bad subject, but I've never heard you talk that way about Chase."

Benny stared at his dad. "You really think I'm in love with Jamie?"

"No, I know you're in love with Jamie. I thought so when I saw the two of you together in the kitchen and the way you defended him on that video, but I knew for sure when I saw the light in your eyes when you talked about him just now." Brian nudged Benny with his elbow. "Welcome to the club."

"The club?" Benny questioned.

"Yeah, the head over heels in love club. Only a very lucky few in the world get to join."

* * * *

Jamie chewed on his thumbnail as he waited for his mother to answer the phone. When it went to voicemail, he sighed. "Hey, it's me. I need to talk to you about what happened with Dad. Could you please call me as soon as you get this?" He ended the call, knowing full well she'd chosen not to answer because she was never without her phone.

He stared at the waterfall for several minutes before getting to his feet. After dropping his phone to the lounger, Jamie took off running and did a cannonball into the pool. He let himself sink to the bottom in an attempt to shut out the world, but all too soon, he was forced to the surface for a much-needed gulp of air.

"Feel better?" Benny asked.

Jamie thought about it. "Yeah, actually, I do."

"Cool." Benny opened the door to the kitchen. "Pool party!" he yelled. "Mind if we join you?"

"I doubt I'm good company right now. My mom's avoiding my call." Jamie barely got the words out before Benny jumped in right beside him. He coughed when he swallowed about a gallon of the chlorinated water. "Jesus, Benny, you created a freaking tidal wave."

"That's my boy," Brian announced from the pool deck. "Unfortunately, a detective should be here any minute, and I don't think the two of you frolicking in the pool is the picture you want to present to him."

Benny easily hoisted Jamie over his shoulder. "Come on, let's get you dry."

Jamie slapped Benny's ass. "I can walk."

"Sure, but where's the fun in that?" Benny replied.

Brian chuckled and Jamie felt his face heat. He couldn't believe Benny had said that right in front of his dad. He was actually thankful when Benny quickly got him into the pool house. "Put me down, Goliath!"

Laughing, Benny set Jamie on his feet. "I would've tossed you to the bed, but we've already ruined one set of sheets today."

Jamie's cock started to harden at the mention of their lovemaking that morning. "I still think it was worth it."

Benny stripped out of his wet clothes. "I don't disagree with you, but I only found one spare set in the linen closet."

Jamie pulled his T-shirt over his head before tossing it to the tiled floor. "I was hoping to talk to my mother before the police got here. I mean, there's really nothing she could've said to change my mind about talking to them, but I feel like I owe her an explanation."

"Even after we talk to the cops, it'll probably take a while before they issue an arrest warrant or anything. Hopefully, your mom'll get in touch soon." Benny grabbed the towel he'd used earlier and wiped himself dry.

"What if she doesn't?" Jamie asked. He knew he'd lost his dad years earlier, even before he'd come out of the closet, but he'd never given up hope that his mother would someday stand up to his father.

Benny wrapped Jamie in a clean towel. "Then she'll be the fool."

Benny began to dry Jamie, but Jamie could tell there was something else Benny wanted to say. "What's wrong?"

Benny shook his head. "There's something I was going to tell you later, but I'm thinking you should hear it now."

Jamie's heart sank. "Okay. Just tell me." He braced himself for the words he'd been waiting to hear since that morning.

"I love you," Benny whispered before smashing his lips against Jamie's.

Jamie opened his mouth and welcomed Benny's tongue inside. The last thing he'd expected was a vow of love from the man he'd pulled into a media nightmare. When they broke for air, Jamie stared up at Benny. "I thought you were going to leave me," he confessed.

"Why would I ever do that? I may play football, but I'm a pretty smart guy." Benny settled his hands on Jamie's hips. "I knew I was falling for you, but it wasn't until I talked to Dad about you that he helped me see what was in my heart. I've been so fucking blind because of what happened with Chase, but I've realized the feelings I had for him aren't nearly as powerful as the love I have for you."

Jamie stood on his tiptoes and kissed Benny's chin. "I love you, too."

"All I want to do is take you to bed, but we've got people waiting on us. Can I get a raincheck for after the pool party?"

"Absolutely." As much as Jamie had enjoyed making love to Benny, he couldn't wait to feel Benny inside him again. He wondered how their sex life would change now that they'd declared their feelings for each other. He smiled to himself because he was anxious to find out.

* * * *

"So let me get this straight. They issued an arrest warrant for my father, but because he's out of state, his lawyer got it quashed? What the hell does that mean?" Jamie asked as he stared out the window in Tony's office. He was waiting for Benny to get back from practice with Brian and Pete. Ethan had gone to the college to sit in on a few of Daniel's classes. Ethan wasn't really interested in art as much as he was college. Jamie still didn't know Ethan's full story, but he got the feeling Ethan had missed out on a lot of living before he'd moved to Cattle Valley.

"It just means that he bonded out of the warrant and won't have to appear until the court date, which isn't even set yet," Tony explained.

Jamie turned to face his new friend. "Aren't you supposed to be in South America again this week?" He hated that his bullshit was affecting the lives of everyone he cared about.

"I'm flying out in a few hours, but I'll only be gone for two days. I told them they had that long to convince me the merger's a good idea," Tony explained.

Even though he knew nothing about Tony's business, Jamie was curious. "Is it a good idea?"

Tony grinned. "It's a great idea, but I don't want to seem too eager." He moved to stand beside Jamie and look out of the window. "I really thought they'd leave after the warrant was issued, but it doesn't appear as though you're going to get your life back until you face them."

"What'll I say to them? The attorneys told me I couldn't discuss the case, so what's left?" Jamie asked.

"Honesty. Go down there and prove to them with your honesty that you're not the monster your dad is making you out to be. Show them your heart. You may not be able to discuss the specifics of the night your dad slapped you, but that's only a small part of your story." Tony rested his hand on Jamie's shoulder. "It's your choice, of course, but I really think that's the only way they'll be satisfied enough to leave you alone."

Jamie thought about it for a few minutes. While he'd love to have Benny at his side when he spoke to the press, it might be better that he wasn't. Benny had suffered enough. "Yeah, okay, I'm not sure what I'll say, so I'd rather not do a formal news conference or anything, but I suppose I could walk down there and say a few words to them."

"When do you want to do it?" Tony asked.

"No time like the present." Jamie walked out of Tony's office. He stopped in the foyer and quickly checked himself in the mirror before opening the front door. The moment he stepped onto the lawn, the reporters started throwing questions at him. He glanced over his shoulder to find Tony a few steps behind him.

I can do this.

When he reached the edge of the lawn, he held up his hands to try to quiet the reporters. When they continued to shout accusations and questions, he took a deep breath and started speaking in a normal voice. If they were smart, they'd figure out they wouldn't get anything if they didn't pipe down.

"My name is Everett James Whitmore III, but the people who care about me call me Jamie." The longer he spoke, the quieter the crowd grew. "I can't talk specifics about the video footage you all saw or the assault case against my father, but a friend suggested I come down here and tell you a little about myself."

Jamie spotted a kind-looking woman in the center of the pack and tried to concentrate on her as he spoke. "Growing up, I always felt different. At first I thought it was because I wasn't allowed to go to school with the kids in my neighborhood, so when I'd come home from boarding school for the summer or school breaks, I had no one to play with. I was isolated in a home with two parents I barely knew."

Jamie swallowed around the lump of emotion in his throat. "I've known since an early age that I was attracted to members of my own sex. At first I thought there was something wrong with me because I'd heard my own father speak so callously about members of the GLBT community for years. My guilt over who I was became so great that I started making excuses as to why I couldn't come home for summer breaks, and sadly, my own parents didn't seem to miss me."

Jamie felt a weight on his shoulder and looked back to see Tony standing just behind him, willing to give him a supporting touch when he needed it. He smiled at Tony before continuing.

"When I graduated from high school, I came out to my mother, but she convinced me that it wasn't the right time to tell my father because he was in the middle of another election campaign. So, I followed her advice and hid who I was for another three years. A month ago, before starting my senior year of college, I finally confessed to my father that I preferred men over women. As you can imagine, the conversation didn't go well. In my family, there is no such thing as unconditional love. Unfortunately, I found that out the hard way."

Jamie took a deep breath. He knew the next part would be the hardest because it exposed the most private part of his life.

"Now, for the first time in my life, I feel truly loved. I didn't recognize it at first because I'd never felt love directed at me, but now that I have it, I'll do anything it takes to keep it. There are people out there who claim homosexuality is a sin, but how can loving someone be wrong? In my mind, a parent not loving a child is the sin. I don't want to run for office or to get involved with politics in any way. All I want, all I've ever wanted, was to be loved for who I am. I want to live a simple life where I can create my pottery and come home to someone I love every night. Please, someone explain to me how that could be considered deviant behavior. I'm not asking for anyone's permission because if I don't have the right to tell you how to live your lives behind closed doors, you certainly don't have the right to discuss what I do when I go home at night."

A few of the reporters threw out questions, but Jamie wasn't about to answer any of them. "This is the last time I'm speaking to the press. If you want to continue to camp out here thinking I'll change my mind about that, let me tell you, I won't. I'm done living my life for people who don't care about me. My happily ever after starts today."

Epilogue

Two years later

"Come on, babe, everyone's waiting on us," Benny hollered from the back porch.

"Be there in a second." Jamie smiled as he finished wrapping the box. For Chase's graduation present, Jamie had made him a swear jar, like the one he'd given Benny so long ago. He would've made one for Chase earlier, but Chase's language wasn't nearly as bad as Benny's. Unfortunately, Chase's newly acquired job as a high school history teacher and coach meant he needed to cut out even the few curse words he used on a regular basis.

"Jamie," Benny called again.

Jamie finished tying the red bow. "I'm coming!" Gift in hand, he turned the lights out in his small studio. Although their house was nothing like Tony's, Benny had made sure Jamie's studio had everything he needed, and Jamie absolutely loved it. He locked the door before holding up the gift. "Sorry, I had to wrap it."

"The cooler's already in the truck." Benny opened the passenger door for Jamie.

"Did you get the pasta salad out of the fridge?" Jamie handed Benny the box while he climbed into the red four-wheel drive pickup.

"Yep." Benny handed back the present before shutting Jamie's door. On his way around the truck, Benny stopped to rub at something on the hood.

Jamie rolled his eyes. Benny had purchased the used dual cab with some of the money they'd been awarded in their civil suits against the news station Bob Keen had once worked for. They definitely hadn't gotten rich off the lawsuits, but they had gotten enough for a nice down payment on their two bedroom house, a used truck for Benny and, of course, Jamie's studio, which had once been the home's garage.

Benny slid in behind the steering wheel. "Mac called and said they were leaving the graduation ceremony, so we should make it to the house right behind them."

"Are we leaving for Cattle Valley right after the party?" Jamie asked, noticing their suitcases in the back seat. He had already given Ethan his graduation present, a vase and a pencil holder for his new office in city hall, so that wasn't an issue, but he wasn't looking forward to a nine-hour drive after spending the afternoon in the warm May sun. He knew how hard Ethan had worked to get his Associate of Applied Science degree from one of the community colleges in Sheridan, but Ethan's graduation party wasn't for three more days.

"Mac and I were talking about it, and we think it'd be best to start out early tomorrow morning. They're taking the bike, so he asked if he could put their bags in here," Benny explained.

"Okay, so why are our suitcases already in the truck?" As much as Jamie loved Benny, he still had trouble figuring out how the man's mind worked sometimes.

"Fiddlesticks! I just thought it would be easier. Okay?"

Jamie couldn't hold back his laugh at Benny's word choice. Since the implementation of the swear jar, Benny had come up with some doozies to use in place of cuss words. He reached over and threaded his fingers through Benny's. "I love you, hon, but that one isn't going to work for you."

Benny grinned and brought Jamie's hand up to his mouth for a soft kiss. "You don't like it? I thought maybe it was time to bring that one back."

"No, you were better off with frack." A thought struck Jamie. "Wait a minute, if you finished packing the bags, did you get my shaving kit, because I'm going to need that in the morning."

Benny growled. "Just drop it."

"What do you mean drop it? It's a simple fiddlesticking question." Jamie didn't understand why Benny was being such an ass about answering him.

"You're right, babe, that word doesn't work," Benny mumbled, still refusing to give Jamie a straight answer.

"Are you trying to piss me off?" Jamie pulled his hand from Benny's, but Benny was quick to capture it again.

"No, I'm trying to do something nice for you, but you're not making it easy. Now, will you please just drop it for now?"

Jamie turned his attention to the view out of the passenger window but left his hand where it was. Maybe Benny was planning to spend the night in a hotel. That would definitely be something Benny would do. He was always doing little things to show Jamie how much he loved him. Who knew such a big man could be so damn romantic? "Fine," he finally mumbled.

* * * *

As soon as they got to the party, Benny carried the cooler into the shaded backyard and set it on the patio. There were a few people already there, including Chase and Mac, who were making out next to the grill. Two years ago the scene would have torn him apart, but Chase and Benny had finally sat down and talked through their problems. Chase had confessed he'd put Benny off because he'd had a feeling things would work out for Benny and Jamie, and Chase had wanted to give him a chance to fall in love with Jamie before they talked.

They had come out of the three-hour conversation as friends again, and Benny had found it had been Chase's friendship that he'd missed the most. Since then, Benny and Mac had also grown closer, and now he considered them among his best friends.

Benny approached the grill and cleared his throat.

Chase and Mac broke their kiss. "Hey," Chase greeted.

"Hey, teach," Benny returned before giving Chase a friendly hug. "Congratulations."

"Thanks." Chase looked around Benny. "Where's your better half?"

"If you mean my *other* half, Jamie's probably unloading the cooler," Benny replied.

"I'll go help him," Chase said. "And don't worry, my lips are sealed." He gave Mac a quick kiss before jogging off toward the house.

"What was that about?" Benny asked.

"Have you talked to Jamie yet about the trip?" Mac began loading the grill with oversized burgers.

Benny shook his head. "Although I almost blew the surprise on the way over. Jamie decided to play twenty questions when he spotted the suitcases in the truck."

"I hear that. Chase caught me packing and asked why I had three new pairs of swim trunks in the suitcase."

"What'd you tell him?" Benny knew Chase was as bad as Jamie when it came to throwing out questions.

"The truth. Well, a partial truth. I told him I was taking him to Kauai for his graduation present and that you, Jamie, Daniel and Tony were coming along. Don't worry, I told him not to say a word to Jamie about it."

Benny thought of the two rings buried in the bottom of his carry-on. "So, how're we doing this? Are we proposing today or would you rather wait until we get to the island?" When he'd mentioned to Mac the idea of whisking Jamie away to Kauai to get married, Mac had asked if they could make it a double ceremony. Seemed Mac had been waiting until Chase graduated to ask him, but Benny had no desire to wait. After all the shit he and Jamie had been through in the last couple of years, Benny had no doubt he and Jamie made a good team, and when Tony had casually offered the use of his vacation home in Kauai, it seemed like the perfect time to make things legal between them.

"Were you able to convince Jamie's mom to come?" Mac asked.

Benny shook his head. "No. She wouldn't take my call."

Although the relationship between Jamie and his father had been severed for good, Jamie still spoke with his mother on occasion. They would probably never have a normal mother-son bond, but at least they were cordial the few times a year they spoke. After the full video had been released, Jamie's father had used his connections to plea bargain his charges down to a misdemeanor offense and had only been fined and sentenced to a few hours of community service. However, even though the courts had gone lenient on him, the Connecticut voters hadn't been as kind.

The civil suits Benny and Jamie had filed against him had come out in their favor to the tune of one hundred thousand dollars each plus court costs. Everett Whitmore II was currently practicing law in his hometown of Hartford and telling everyone he knew that his son had sabotaged his career as part of some gay agenda global conspiracy. Yeah, that little news tidbit still made Benny laugh.

"That's too bad. My best friend Skeet'll meet us there but his sister Evie and her family can't come because she's on bed rest with her most recent pregnancy," Mac said.

"Dad, Ethan and Pete are meeting us in L.A. What about your boy and Chase's mom?" Benny knew how pleased Mac was that his son, Jackson, was moving to town to attend college.

"Yep. I think Gwen'll be on the same flight with your crew from Sheridan. Jackson's meeting us in Los Angeles. He can't wait to fly on a private plane." Mac gestured to a large platter. "Hold that out for me. I think this first batch's done."

Benny did as asked, his mind on Jamie and when to tell him what he had planned for the next ten days. Ten fucking days sharing Tony's vacation house with the entire extended family. To most people, it sounded like a nightmare, but to Benny, it sounded like the best honeymoon ever. "I don't think I can wait until we get there, but I don't want to make it some big thing either. I think I'll just pull him aside and do it my own way."

"That's fine with me. Just let me know when, so I can do the same with Chase," Mac suggested.

"Will do," Benny agreed.

* * * *

Finished with the clean-up, Jamie joined the small group of their closest friends that were left on the patio. It was only a little after three, but most of the crowd had moved on to other graduation parties.

"Is Chase still working?" Mac asked.

Jamie settled into Benny's lap. "Not really." He yawned. "He said he wanted to make sure he packed everything."

"I'd better go help him," Mac said as he got to his feet.

"Well, that's our cue." Tony stood and held his hand out to Daniel. "Ready, love?"

Daniel nodded.

"Do I smell?" Jamie asked.

Daniel laughed before giving Jamie a kiss on the cheek. "No, Tony has to leave on another trip, so he's got some packing of his own to do."

"See you when we get back from Cattle Valley," Jamie called as Tony and Daniel left hand in hand. He snuggled against Benny. "It was a nice party."

"Yeah it was," Benny agreed. "I was thinking. Instead of leaving in the morning, I'd rather take off today."

Jamie groaned. "Why? We've got plenty of time to get there."

Benny leaned to the side and started digging around in his front pocket. "Because the sooner we get there, the sooner we can get married."

Jamie stilled. "What?"

Benny held out two simple platinum wedding bands. "I know I'm still in school, but I don't want to wait to make you mine forever. Marry me, Jamie."

"What!" Jamie shrieked. "You want to get married? Now?" He felt his breathing pick up and was afraid he'd start to hyperventilate. Each time they'd had to sit in a courtroom in the last two years he'd expected Benny to break up with him, and here they were, finally on the other side of all the legal nightmares, and Benny actually wanted to marry him? "Fuck," Jamie wheezed.

"Breathe, babe." Benny rubbed Jamie's back. "All you have to do is say yes. Everything else's been taken care of."

"Yes!" Jamie wrapped his arms around Benny's neck and kissed him. "Yes! Yes! Yes!" He sobered when he realized something. "Did you want to get married in Cattle Valley? Is that why you're in such a hurry to get there?"

"As much as I love Cattle Valley, I thought we were due for a much-needed vacation, so we're all going to Kauai for the ceremony and honeymoon," Benny said between kisses.

"Who's we?" Jamie asked.

"Everyone we care the most about. Mac's inside now asking Chase the same question I asked you. He and I have planned a double ceremony at Tony's house on the beach."

Jamie's head was spinning. He was going to Kauai to get married, but more importantly, not only had Benny not been scared away by all the drama in Jamie's life, but he actually wanted to be with him forever. "Can we leave now?" he asked. "Crap. I should've packed different clothes."

Benny chuckled. "Relax. I told you, I've taken care of everything. Well, Daniel had a helping hand in picking out something for you to wear at the ceremony."

Jamie moved around until he was straddling Benny's lap. "I love you so much."

Benny squeezed Jamie's ass. "I love you, too, babe."

* * * *

Jamie's eyes filled with tears the moment he stepped foot out of the sprawling mansion. Soft white lights wound their way up a cluster of palm trees flanked by pots of tropical flowers. *Damn.* The tranquil beach they'd sunbathed on earlier had been transformed into a romantic hideaway meant for only him and the people he loved most. He squeezed Benny's hand. "It's breathtaking."

"You like it?" Benny asked, shuffling his weight from foot to foot.

Jamie gazed up at his nervous groom-to-be. "It's so much more than I expected." He lifted Benny's hand to his lips and kissed it.

"Good." Benny drew Jamie to a stop in front of a middle-aged Hawaiian woman. "Have you ever been lei'd by a woman?"

"Nope, it'll be a first." A sweet scent filled Jamie's nostrils as he bent to accept the orchid and ti leaf lei. "Thank you," he told the woman.

Jamie held on to Benny's hand as the petite woman draped one of the fragrant necklaces around Benny's neck. "You look good in flowers."

Benny grinned. "You think?" He preened, prompting a chuckle from Jamie.

"I know." Jamie moved toward the small group gathered in front of the palms.

Benny bent low and whispered, "Daniel said these pants would be perfect for the ceremony, but I don't think he took into account the effect you have on my cock."

Jamie glanced down, expecting to see a bulge in Benny's loose-fitting, white linen pants, and was slightly disappointed. "Fortunately for them, unfortunately for me, your shirt covers your mighty staff of manhood."

Benny was still laughing when they joined the group. As a unit, Brian, Pete and Ethan surged forward to wrap their arms around Benny and Jamie.

"I couldn't be happier. I've always wanted more children, and now I have another son," Brian said in Jamie's ear.

Jamie hugged Brian tighter when he realized how much he'd needed to hear those words. "Thank you for raising such a kind-hearted son, and for accepting me despite the drama that surrounded me."

Brian kissed Jamie's forehead. "How could I not accept the man who has so completely captured my son's heart?"

Jamie briefly wondered what it would have been like to be raised by such an understanding man. He pushed the thought away as he was turned and enveloped in Pete's embrace.

Once the pre-wedding greetings were finished, Benny and Jamie moved to stand to one side of the minister, while Mac and Chase mirrored their position. They had all agreed on a basic ceremony in front of their family and friends, with a private ceremony between each couple after the legalities were taken care of.

By the time the minister gave them permission to kiss, Jamie's cheeks hurt from smiling. He squeaked when Benny picked him up off the sand and crushed their mouths together. With their audience forgotten, Jamie opened and accepted Benny's tongue as he felt the ridge of Benny's erection press against him.

When Benny finally set him back onto his feet, the private words he'd been dying to say to his new husband came pouring out of him. "Growing up, I felt like a burden to the people who were supposed to love me, so I gave up on the concept that life could ever be the fairy tale I read about in books and saw in movies."

Benny cupped Jamie's face in his big hands as his eyes filled with emotion.

"Then I saw you in a bar, and you captured my attention so thoroughly that I told myself I didn't care that you were in love with someone else because all I needed from you was a crumb of something real. I was drowning in a sea of self-pity, and I knew in my gut, you could be my life preserver—even if for only one night. I had no intention of falling in love, but once you came to my rescue that night of the pool party, I had to give you the one thing no one had ever asked from me."

Jamie wiped Benny's tears as they trailed down his cheeks. "You've held my heart in the palm of your hand for over two years, and you've shown me time and time again that it wasn't my heart that was lacking, but the hands that had never reached out to accept all that I had to give. I love you, and I vow to be worthy of your love and trust until the day I die."

"Oh, baby," Benny whispered as he leaned over to give Jamie another hungry kiss. "You're so much better with words than I'll ever be, but I need you to know that you've filled a space in me that I didn't even know existed. I've always been lucky to have parents who've loved me unconditionally, but it's different when someone *chooses* to love you as completely as you do me."

Benny brushed his thumbs over Jamie's wet cheeks just as Jamie had done for him. "I wish I could promise you the world. Unfortunately all I have is myself to give, but I swear on my life that you'll get every ounce of me until the day I die."

Jamie shook his head the moment Benny stopped talking. "You've already given me the world. You just haven't realized that yet."

* * * *

After a beautiful sunset ceremony and too many glasses of celebratory champagne, Benny fell into bed with his new husband. Their vows to each other hadn't been meant for others, but by the time they were done speaking, there hadn't been a dry eye on the beach. "I've been waiting all day to get you back in bed," he said, pulling Jamie astride him.

Jamie dripped lube down Benny's cock. "You had me two hours ago in the laundry room, right after the ceremony," Jamie pointed out.

"Yeah, but that was fucking. Now it's time to make love." Benny reached up and placed his hand on the back of Jamie's neck before pulling him down for a deep kiss. He thrust his tongue inside Jamie's mouth before rolling them over. Once he was on top, he wasted no time in pushing his length inside the man he loved.

Jamie broke the kiss. "You feel so good, honey."

Benny groaned in reply as he slowly pumped in and out of Jamie's heated body. "I love you," he whispered for about the hundredth time that day.

"Not as much as I love you," Jamie whispered back.

A loud banging started in the adjoining bedroom, quickly followed by several moans of pleasure.

Benny stilled as Jamie started to giggle. "Oh my God. Are they trying to embarrass me to death?" Benny couldn't believe he'd agreed to share a house with nine other people. "It's my honeymoon!" he shouted to the adjacent wall.

Benny distinctly heard his father's laughter, but the noise didn't lessen. "I'm gonna kill him tomorrow. Hell, I'm going to murder all three of them."

Jamie wrapped his legs around Benny's torso. "At least now I know where you get your stamina from."

"Gross." Benny didn't want to think about his dad's sex life while he had his dick buried in Jamie.

"It's not gross," Jamie argued. "I think it's heartwarming that your dad's so happy with Pete and Ethan. Would you rather he be alone like Chase's mom?"

"Of course not, and I'm happy for him, too but that doesn't mean I want to hear him fucking." Benny tried to block out the continued sounds of his father having sex and focused all his attention on Jamie. He still didn't understand why his dad needed two men to make him happy, but he'd come to terms with it long ago. "You're the only man I'll ever need in my bed."

"That's good, because I'd never share you anyway." Another loud series of grunts from the other room had Jamie giggling once again.

"This is war," Benny proclaimed as he thrust his hips. "Fuck, you feel good," he shouted, loud enough for the entire house to hear.

Jamie stopped laughing long enough to reply, "Harder, Benny. God, you're so big!"

It was Benny's turn to laugh as he continued to screw the hell out of his husband. He pressed his hand against the headboard and purposely banged it against the wall with every thrust of his hips.

A loud thump against the wall drew Benny's attention. It seemed his father didn't care to know what was going on in Benny's bed.

"We win," Jamie said.

"Yes we do," Benny agreed, knowing he'd won the greatest prize of all.

About the Author

An avid reader for years, one day Carol Lynne decided to write her own brand of erotic romance. Carol juggles between being a full-time mother and a full-time writer. These days, you can usually find Carol either cleaning jelly out of the carpet or nestled in her favorite chair writing steamy love scenes.

Carol loves to hear from readers. You can find her contact information, website details and author profile page at http://www.pride-publishing.com.

PUBLISHING